THE ANGEL SHIP

Published by Hellgate Press

(An imprint of L&R Publishing, LLC)

Hellgate Press

PO Box 3531

Ashland, OR 97520

email: info@hellgatepress.com

Interior & Cover Design: L. Redding

Front cover painting: "Dunkirk Beaches, 1940" by Richard Eurich

Cataloging In Publication Data is available from the publisher upon request.

ISBN: 978-1-55571-960-9

Printed and bound in the United States of America

First edition 10 9 8 7 6 5 4 3 2 1

THE
ANGEL
SHIP

KJ KENNELLY

Hellgate Press   Ashland, Oregon

For Peter, an intrepid voyager and kindred spirit.
May your shipmates be loyal and your winds fair.

Prologue

O N MAY 24, 1940, the British Expeditionary Force (BEF) and Allied troops are pinned against the coast near the French port of Dunkirk. The Germans are ten miles away and advancing. There appears to be no escape. There are 400,000 men to be evacuated. Available warships draw too much water to get near the beaches, so smaller craft are needed. Volunteers come forward with their boats. It is one of the greatest rescues of all time by this fleet of small vessels designated "The Little Ships of Dunkirk."

The heroism of these volunteers becomes legendary. This deliverance of 338,000 men safely back to England to fight again expedites victory in World War II.

"As long as the English tongue survives," said the *New York Times*, "the word Dunkerque will be spoken with reverence."

The historian Walter Lord said, "To the British, Dunkirk symbolizes a generosity of spirit, a willingness to sacrifice for the common good… to the French, a bitter defeat, to the Germans, opportunity forever lost."

Marie Celine, also called "The Angel Ship," was one of the "Dunkirk Little Ships."

ONE

Marie Celine

*H*ER NAME WAS *Marie Celine* and my parents built her. She was fifty feet long, a staysail schooner, elegant and sea-kindly. She was launched in 1936, and we were going to sail round the world. Then the war happened.

My, such a long time. Sixty years. A blind longing. A dream of *Marie Celine* coming back to me. That lost part of my life coming back. They all said: "You can't go home again," but I had a chance to return. I had to take it.

My, such a long time.

Sixty years ago I hid under the foresail bag on the bow of *Marie Celine* as she headed across the Dover Strait to help evacuate the British Expeditionary Force. I was fourteen. All so well remembered— as if it were yesterday. Black memories. Black dive bombers. Black thunder.

The *Marie Celine* was in the first convoy of Little Ships that left for Dunkirk from Ramsgate, 2200 hours, Wednesday, May 29, 1940. Outside the Ramsgate breakwater, the Channel was tranquil, like smoked glass against a curtain of low clouds. Putts and sputters of engines, fluttering sails, shouts, and whistles refracted off the dense atmosphere. Diesel fuel, coal, and petrol fumes mixed with iodine and the fishy odours of the sea. The escorting motorboat, *Triton*, waited for us. Her skipper's bullhorn echoed off the fog, "All you ships close up now and follow me. There'll be no Stukas or Heinkels tonight. Not with clouds this thick."

And *Marie Celine* headed out under diesel power, her double-reefed mainsail up for stability. We towed two long boats with two-man rowing stations and two ship's lifeboats, each capable of holding maximum, about sixteen men.

I gripped the samson posts as *Marie Celine's* bow cut through the glassy water. She gently lifted and rolled with wakes from the bigger boats. Ahead in the vapour were about ten boats, mostly escorts. Dutch barges, a Portsmouth–Isle of Wight ferry, tugs, and a few open motor launches. Looking astern, I saw a flotilla of lifeboats under tow by another Dutch barge, sailing yachts like ours, and a string of Royal National Lifeboats towed by a couple of Thames excursion boats. Herring drifters, oyster dredgers, and cockle boat fleets from Leigh-on-Sea sailed out from the estuaries alongside single-mast fishing smacks and cabin cruisers in Bristol condition. The convoy stretched as far as I could see until it smudged into the horizon.

A destroyer moved towards *Marie Celine*. As she came abeam, I could make out the name on her quarter: *Malcolm*. Her engines hummed. The decks were laden with shadow soldiers against a dusky night. Tin hats like a field of domes. Rifles, slung over their shoulders, stabbed the night.

A Thames excursion boat passing on our port had BBC on the wireless. A folk song, *Widecome Fair,* rang out. It was a well-known ballad about a farmer who had lent his grey mare to a neighbour who wanted to go to the fair. He promised the farmer he would take good care of the mare. Instead, he abused her and loaded her down with all of his mates. The mare died of the weight. On moonlit nights the mare was seen running the skies of Devon, moaning under the heavy load. I gazed back at the figures on the *Malcolm's* decks. I wondered if they were feeling that weight of war and defeat, those silent soldiers against the night.

At that moment, artillery crumped in the distance. I saw a faint smoky-red reflection off the sky ahead.

After the *Malcolm* passed, her wake hit. The wave sent small craft off in different directions like so many wood chips. *Marie Celine* heaved, rolling violently, dipping her rails in the sea. Dad cursed from the helm. I lost my hold and tumbled down the deck into the boots of Mallory McCay. He huffed, "What in hell's name do you think you're doing here?" Mal's carrot-hair stood up like a brush on his egghead. Freckles blotched his pink skin. He was wearing his dress Royal Navy, all the brass buttons gleaming. My bully neighbor looked impressive and older, but that made no difference to me. I grew up with Mal.

Mallory McCay was a lowly Royal Navy sub-lieutenant. He'd seen action in the North Sea and got commissioned. And Mallory-Mad-Mal McCay was only sixteen. A big lad with no fear. His body looked stuffed into a uniform made for a normal-sized soldier. I knew Mal lied when he went in, as many of my schoolmates did. If it weren't for my parents, I would be in blues with brass shining everywhere. After all, I was actually taller than Mal, just not as thick. And I had more hair on my legs. And there he was on my boat, running the show.

The Admiralty had ordered their own to man the civilian boats going on this mission. Dad would hear nothing of that. But Mal had asked for our boat and Dad welcomed him. Family.

Dad looked splendid that night wearing his blue jacket of the Royal London Yacht Club, khaki trousers, and a tin helmet. He hovered over the wheel, tugged at his white mustache, and shook his head. "Colley, you were supposed to stay in school with the other lads." He slid open the binnacle. The red compass light sprayed his long face. His eyes flickered at me from under the deep cover of tangled brows, "Go below and help your mother." He checked his course, "East-south-east." Then he closed the binnacle cover and said to Mal, "Check and see that no one has lost his way. I know the compasses on some of those pleasure boats have never been corrected. We're under orders to follow the convoy. I think they may be off course."

Mal swept the horizon with his binoculars. "There are mixed messages, Doctor Neville.

At 2130 the signals said to instruct all personnel boats not to close

Dunkirk harbour, for it's completely blocked; we were to head for eastern beaches to collect troops. Now I've got a signal from that destroyer to port. He's saying the entrance to Dunkirk harbour is practicable."

Dad said, "We'll have to stand by."

I hesitated, wanting desperately to be part of it all—to be on deck. It was always Dad and me. Now I was being sent below? I gave him a defiant look. He raised his brows, "Do as I say, lad!"

When I reached the bottom of the companionway steps, the galley steamed. A large stew pot foamed brown liquid, spitting onto the stove, and another pot bubbled with potatoes. The stew and potatoes gave off an earthy and slightly urine-tinged odour. I remembered that smell from the back lanes of town. Mutton. A copper on the back burner simmered boiled tea, so black it had a slick on it. We never drank our tea that way. And mutton? I thought it tasted like piss!

In the orange flicker of oil lamps, Mum turned from stoking the coal stove. With her grey hair pinned up into a knot, her wide face looked like a moon. Those rosy English cheeks glowed with heat from the stove; sweat came down her temples. Her eyes burned with a scary light and narrowed, "So! Dad knew about this?"

"No, Mum. Dad didn't know a thing. I swear!"

She paused and slid the palms of her hands down the sides of her apron. I knew I was going to catch it. I stood almost a head over her, but she had strong, tight arms. She let out a breath. "*Marie Celine* is having company to tea. These boys will be hungry and thirsty. We're taking them off the beaches tonight. We're taking our house to war."

An uneasy feeling had been lingering over my country. There had been no public announcement of evacuation, but Mum knew. She was a sister at St. John's Hospital. Whether she was allowed to be aboard, or whether she stowed away as I did, I will never know.

Mum and I worked together through the night. We peeled onions, carrots, and potatoes.

In addition to our full copper water tanks, cans of water were made fast on the teak and holly cabin sole. The Admiralty dropped off cans of water, cases of Bully Beef, corned beef, Bovril, HP brown sauce and sherry. "Sherry?" Mum queried. "Why sherry, I wonder…" Dad's cache of single malts lay up in the bin behind the counter by the galley. The Admiralty had ordered the boats to lighten up, to toss our non-essential gear. We had no time for that. Besides, our ship could carry a great deal of weight. That's how Mum and Dad designed her—a heavy-built cruiser.

Marie Celine was Mum's castle, her home—the dream and joy she and Dad had saved and worked for all these years. Dad laid her oak backbone in Philip and Son boatyard, Dartmouth, Devon, and she grew into a fifty-foot schooner. She was an exotic creature in England. Schooner rigs were rare; but in Nova Scotia, where Dad was born, a schooner was the best rig to have.

My dad was a doctor, but his passion was designing yachts. He was born and raised in Lunenburg, Nova Scotia. His father was a doctor in that prosperous fishing and shipbuilding town. Lunenburg Bay was a forest of spars in those days. Dad spent every free moment down at the bustling docks, or at Smith and Rhuland boatyard. At night, instead of doing schoolwork, he built model ships. After school, Dad went to the shore and tested his sailing boats. Determined that the boy get a proper education, and to wean him off boats, Dad's parents banished him to an English boarding school at the age of sixteen.

At seventeen, he and a couple of mates joined up to defend England and Canada in World War One. It was after the war that he finished school in England and became a doctor. Before, after, and sometimes during his workdays, Dad designed yachts, sailed yachts, and later, built yachts. He designed some formidable boats in those days, *Marie Celine* being the queen of all of them. Dad believed she was the most perfect deep-water cruising yacht ever built. She was named after my Acadian grandmother.

We had lived aboard since I was born. Mum would not let me or my mates below without taking off our shoes. She polished all the raised oak and walnut panels. And not one fingerprint dulled our brass, copper, and bronze. That night it looked like a barracks. Mutton fog permeated wood; it steamed up the brass fixtures and Dutch tiles of our saloon. Wool blankets, cork life preservers, extra sweaters, oilskins, Dad's medical bags, and rolls of spare bandages littered our plush green settees. And not one gun. And all the time I heard the shelling getting closer. When I could, I opened a scupper and peeked out. The sky throbbed with flashes of red, white, and yellow light that outlined a black battlement of clouds. In the pre-dawn, the interior of *Marie Celine* bled to crimson, and artillery thunder shook the hull of Mum's beautiful boat. Exhausted, Mum dropped off for a moment in the pilot berth, under the companionway. I climbed up the companionway steps and wedged into the hatch, facing Dad. Shepherding, Mum was up and right behind me. Dad was talking to Mal, "Dunkirk. Mark: 0500 hours. Off starboard forequarter. Doesn't look right. I believe we need to be at La Panne. Or Malo-les-Bains, along the dunes." Dad's face radiated the inferno that surrounded us. His white mustache and hair, fringing the edge of his helmet, blazed red. The sea was on fire.

We had to be more than a mile off Dunkirk. It was my first experience of gunfire. Salvos from a German shore battery came one way, and our ships answered back over our masthead.

The noise thrummed and cracked right through my body.

Mal sat in the cockpit with Dad. Fixed on the scene ahead, his young hairless face shone bright rose in the glow. "There appear to be some guns outside of town. Bloody guns! We didn't expect guns to be this close. Jerries' artillery can't possibly have the range!" He raised his binoculars and searched the shoreline.

I took glasses from the rack beside me and adjusted the lenses. The city of Dunkirk that I knew as a child, with its bathing houses and vacation villas, was ablaze. The oil tank farm had been bombed and spewed billows of black smoke and flame. Bathing huts, food stalls, and boardwalks along the beach were burning. There were two long piers, called "moles", built out into the sea before the port entrance, like breakwaters. Broken ships were all around the port entrance and out to the moles. Dead ships jutted out of the sea like charred bone fragments of shattered skeletons. Prows, bows, sterns up, wedges of wide paddle wheelers, and spars crammed the entrance. Ship's furniture, bulkheads, tin hats, dead men. Dead men floated all around us. I thought I would be sick, but my mouth was dry from fear and my stomach heaved painfully.

An Isle of Man ferry, heading into Dunkirk to pick up troops, had just been hit and split in half. I heard Mal and Dad shouting, questioning the source of the explosion. They didn't know if it was a torpedo from a Schnellboote or a magnetic mine. Suddenly the water all round was aflame. The blast sent us surfing on confused waves. Dad was wrestling with the helm, zigzagging to avoid being hit. "Watch for debris lads. I can't do everything!"

Cloud reflection shone on fiery stumps in the water. I had to focus the glass on them, for the bomb surge was bringing them our way; they could puncture *Marie's* hull. I wish I hadn't looked. Those blackened stumps were bodies of men covered with oil, on fire, still floating in their life jackets and life belts, their burning arms raised, signaling for help. The urge to cry out rattled me. I was not going to cry. Holding my breath, I pressed my fist against my mouth. But sobs were swelling my chest and rising to my throat, choking me. I started up the steps to help, to bring them aboard, our men, save them. Mum pressed her face in my back and pulled me down the ladder by the hem of my shirt. She held me there on the steps. "They are gone, love. Gone to heaven." Explosive sobs jolted my body against hers. "Gone to heaven, love." After a bit, I got my breath back and finally my head cleared.

On deck I heard Mal railing, "Oh God, oh God, God!"

Mum observed, "Mal's grabbed his torch. Flashing to the naval ships standing offshore. His hands are shaking. I hope they can read his signals." She eased me up a step and together we watched.

The thunder of artillery clapped from the shore and was returned by our war ships. The sea looked like red oatmeal and smelled of oil so strong it was hard to breathe. Our escort ships had scattered. Spouts of water erupted on all sides of us.

Mal's torch blinked. He repeated, incredulous, "Shell fire from ashore. Germans are too damn close. They don't have their range yet, but God-knows, they will soon. They will soon." In seconds Mal caught a flashing message from a destroyer waiting offshore. "It's no good here, Doctor. They say we're supposed to be at the dunes near La Panne. Can you do it Doctor Neville? Do you know how to get there?"

Dad opened the compass binnacle, checked his headings, tapped the throttle up and turned the helm. "No worries. Hold on, lads."

TWO

La Panne

*I*T WAS HARD to tell in the mist, but I think we may have been one of the first small vessels at the beaches off La Panne. The Admiralty said there would be soldiers there to be ferried to the naval ships in deeper waters. We still had the luck of the weather and no Luftwaffe. At full dawn, Dad had me up on the bow taking soundings with the lead line. The sky and the sea were like mauve sheets. I heard a low roar. I couldn't make out the sound; it came from the beaches. I tossed the lead into the water and counted the knots in the line and called back, "Three fathoms, mark. Two, mark." I watched the shore. I could see lorries, motorcycles, haversacks, and rifles strewn about the water's edge. But I saw no soldiers, only dark spots on the dunes. The rumbling roar continued.

"That's as far as she goes, lads," Dad called out. Mal and I tossed the forward anchor into the sandy bottom. Dad backed off and set her right. The fog cleared enough for us to see the spots on the beach moving. I realized that the roar was the moan of the wounded, the shouts and the murmurs of thousands of men. Soldiers crawled out of bomb craters and off the dunes. In a confused mass they made their way to the water. Muddied, caked with blood and sand, they waded out. Some carried bloodied and bandaged mates on their backs. They looked like walking dead men. I was shaking and fearful.

Mal put his arm over my shoulder. "Shit," he said, "is this what our army has come to?" Overwhelmed, Mal and I fixed on the spectacle.

"Lads. Lads!" I heard Dad call, as if from another world, "Let's press on!"

Marie Celine's draft was too deep; we couldn't get in close enough. Some of the troops began to swim with their gear still strapped on. They didn't look as if they could make it. Dad quickly untied the longboat and handed the painter to Mal. I shipped a lifeboat, tossed in the oars, and jumped in. I had another set of oarlocks and oars, but I was only taking one set until we got our bearings ashore. Mal was ahead of me rowing; he could hold more than ten men. He also had another set of oarlocks and oars.

Mal hit the shallows by the beach first; the soldiers swamped his boat, which capsized, and the oars floated off.

Soldiers surrounded me. I yelled, "Keep off! Stand clear!" They grabbed onto my rails trying to board, pulling the boat and me under the water. Some men tried to help, but they didn't know anything about the water. "Help me!" I screamed. "Get under here. Grab the rail. Pull, pull, pull! Up and over." No one heard. They were trampling me. I was invisible. In the confusion, I thought I heard Mum calling my name. My boat was completely swamped. I was sure I'd lost her. A couple of men tried bailing with their helmets.

Dad tossed out a line with a cork lifesaver on the end. A few of the soldiers were able to grab it and work their way along the rope to the boat. My parents helped them up the rope ladders. And I was still left with a swarm of desperate soldiers.

At that moment, a jet-haired, thin, fragile-looking lieutenant came wading out to me.

Natty, in army uniform, all his brass shined. His face was clean-shaven and chapped. His voice boomed over the confusion, "Rutherford, here. Fifth Medium Regiment. Royal Artillery. Chappies get a sea unit going!" Rutherford, the only officer I saw, seemed to bring the men together. We dumped the water, righted the lifeboat, and Rutherford organized one group of soldiers to hold the boat while the others boarded in orderly fashion. These men would be the next to leave and another team would come in. How we managed to pack so many men on the bench seats and the floorboards was a miracle. There was so little freeboard, one shift would certainly capsize the boat. I was on the center bench with one soldier beside me on the other oar, learning how to row. I coached, "In and out, in and out…one, two, in and out…"

We reached the side of *Marie Celine* and I held on to the rope ladders. A couple of the soldiers scrambled up, throwing the boat out of balance. "Stop! Don't all leave from the same place. You'll toss us in the sea! Slow down!" This time I think they listened for they did snap to and send one man up at a time. Others did not move at all. They stared; the tired faces went blank. I said, "Up, go up the ladders! We're taking you home! Now, one, two, upsy-daisy!"

Balancing in the boat, I boosted while Mum and Dad pulled. All aboard. I went back for the next lot. Mal was up and rowing out with a full load. Rutherford manned the second set of oars, yelling, "Cheer up, lads. You're going home. To hell with the Germans!"

"To hell with the Germans!" the men cheered.

"To hell with the Germans!" a naked soldier shouted. Rutherford grabbed him and another soldier threw a greatcoat over him.

On my next trip to *Marie Celine*, I saw Mum making a face. The stench from the men was acute. She shouted, "Get out your mess kits. Come to the companionway." She dashed ahead and slipped below. Anxiously, I followed the men mobbing the companionway. I saw some climb in from the midship hatch, some squeezed down the ladder to the forward crews' quarters—my stateroom. They rushed aft to the main saloon, crowding Mum. She was pinned. Tin cups and bowls were thrust at her from all directions. I saw confusion and fear on Mum's face. These men were starving. The rusty-nail smell of dried blood and the sour odour of urine, feces, unwashed bodies, and cigarettes clogged the air. I offered to go below, but she shook her head.

Helping new soldiers aboard, I looked down the main hatch. With-

out looking up, Mum ladled stew, water, and boiled tea into an assortment of containers. Filling one tin bowl, she noticed she had ladled stew
over a bloody field bandage dangling in the dish. The young man pulled
up his wrapped hand, sucked the bandage dry, and flipped it back
around his hand with his teeth. His wet brown eyes followed each ladled
splash of stew with wonder. I watched Mum turn her head away and
take a deep breath. Then her tear-filled eyes met his, as she smiled and
slopped an extra ladle in his bowl. "And that's one to go home on, love."

Dad managed to keep a small lot of the men below, low, on the cabin
sole, to balance the weight in the boat. The others, topsides, were to lie
down or sit. He attended those who needed medical help. "I hadn't realized there would be such chaos. Such chaos, such chaos," he muttered
to himself as he moved from soldier to soldier with his medical bag.

When he was not tending soldiers, Dad helped Mum. She worked
on, breathless, brave, weepy at times, sharp and cranky other times. Dad
went below and said to Mum, "We're full. We are too low in the water
as it is. It's been slow going; next trip we'll be more efficient. But there
were more soldiers coming on the beaches, last time I looked." He lifted
another jug of water up on the sink board and poured boiled potatoes
and gravy into a bucket and started up the ladder. He paused, "This
whole process is too slow. Messages say Jerry's moving down the coast."

"What's that mean in time, love?" I heard Mum ask.

"Time?" He took in her look. "Could be a day, maybe two. Jerry is
already on the outskirts of Dunkirk. The British Expeditionary Force
and French are holding them off." He let out a tired sigh, backed
down the ladder, and kissed her forehead, his lips lingering there
longer than usual.

Mum glanced up at his white-whiskered face and intelligent eyes. "I
hope we make it through."

He touched her cheek. "Oh, we'll make it through all right. We'll
win this war. Then, we'll be sailing the South Pacific. Colley will be fishing from his canoe. And you?" He chucked her on the chin. "You'll be
dressed in a sarong, suntanned, bringing me my Glen Scotia in a co-

conut shell." He continued up the ladder, "Right now, we've got a man in every crack of this boat. We are putting up some sails for extra power."

A navy launch bumped to port and unloaded small stores of Navy cocoa, bread, tinned beef, and jugs of water. Mum worked on making sandwiches of corned beef and Coleman's mustard. She added Bovril, HP sauce, and water to the stew. She also tended the wounded below.

On deck it was hard for Mal and me to move about getting the sails up. The engine kicked in for Dad, and we got the foresails up and shook the reefs out of the main without tangling anyone in the lines. *Marie Celine* turned offshore. We were tense; what with the weight, the easterly breeze, and the currents, if she decided to flounder or balk, we could be dead. Sitting ducks. Would we get a way on? We felt her shudder and remain perfectly still.

Mal bounded from port rail to starboard rail, "What? Hell! We've run aground!" The soldiers' voices dimmed.

Dad stroked *Marie Celine's* cockpit coaming, reached over, patted her sides and said in a tender voice, so the passengers would not hear, "Come darling, love of my life, Old Thing. You have lives to save."

Marie Celine shuddered again, creaked and moaned, as her keel dragged the bottom, and she gradually moved off the wind. Gaining speed, she headed out and into the Channel. There was a breath of wind. The diesel chunked away. Clouds began to thin. For the first time we noticed the odd assortment of boats that were with us, ferrying BEF.

The soldiers aboard were beginning to look less haggard. Atmosphere lightened. Some flat on the decks in oblivious sleep. Others smoked and chatted with their mates and shared bottles of sherry passed around by Mum. Some curled up in balls around the mast and anchor wind-lass, anywhere they could fit, and slept. Some got sick on the deck.

"Look Mal, wind for our lady. I see patches of blue." I felt infused with triumph.

Mal frowned up at the sky. "Man, you don't want that! Clear skies, we get Stukas! Wind, we get waves so we can't get chaps off the beach!"

That first trip, overloaded with BEF, was long. Currents were strong and *Marie Celine* made a slow, but gentle headway for the waiting destroyer, *Oriole*. Bombs were going off by the Mole, fires belched into the sky. So far, we had been free of enemy aircraft near our part of the coast, but at that moment, we heard the roar of bombers headed for our beaches.

By the time we returned and set anchor off La Panne, the beach had a new appearance. There were piles of dead soldiers, eight deep, along the dunes. Dead fish floated everywhere: herring, mackerel, sprats. The stench was choking me. Then the real horror began. Bumping up alongside the boat and lining the shore were khakied corpses. Poor devils, they'd waited to go home. Mal and I rowed on ashore, pushing through the dead. We found Lieutenant Rutherford heading up the construction of a jetty built of abandoned lorries, scavenged lumber from a lumberyard, cable, rope, and decking torn from stranded ships for a plank walkway.

Rutherford bristled, "I don't know much about soldiering, but even I could see that shore detail wasn't working. Went round the dunes, found a company of Royal Engineers. We rolled the lorries out, lined them up side-by-side, shot the tires flat, loaded sandbags on the frames.

Have a look: we've even got ourselves a walkway with a rope railing." Rutherford hustled away and frisked at the sides of the soldiers.

The jetty company worked all night, while Mal and I and all the other small vessels ferried soldiers. The first day, we small ships took about 14,000 off the beaches. The next day, after the jetty construction and with the arrival of more small craft, we got nearly 30,000 off. Those two days we saw calm in the Channel.

The following day the skies cleared, and for the first time I heard the screaming whistles of the Stukas as they swarmed out of the rising sun towards us.

THREE

The Last Days

*V*EE PATTERNS OF aircraft etched the dawn sky. They were flying in at high altitude. I was on the beach with Mal and Rutherford, who were organizing the troops for an orderly evacuation. Small craft crept in to load men. Overnight, thousands of battered, dazed, and weary BEF had arrived on the beach. Columns of men, eight thick, led from shore into the sea. The soldiers in front were up to their waists, and some up to their shoulders in water. Another line snaked out from the dunes to the lorry-jetty. Lying at the water's edge was a soldier, not far from our launching area. He was waving and pointing to his legs. I hesitated. An officer with a megaphone barked, "You there, get on with the evacuation. We need to get the ones that can fight off the beaches."

Many of the men were drunk from French wine found in the cellars in which they had been hiding. Mal towered over most of the soldiers. He pushed, shoved and yelled as he dragged them off the dunes. "Shape up, you the Army! Do you want your countrymen to see you like this?"

One half-naked soldier sat in the sand holding a baby doll. Trickles of blood had dried on his face, "It's not fair. I've got a wife. Children." Mal rushed to him and yanked his elbow. The man's arms tightened.

He sobbed, "I can't leave me baby." Mal lifted the man to his feet and shoved him. "Tears won't win this war. I'll give you three to queue up." Mal cocked his rifle. The soldier stumbled away, dragging the doll by its skirt.

The drone of aircraft engines silenced the masses. Hushed, the men watched the formation.

One of the soldiers in the columns yelled, "Finally! Spitfires! It's about time, RAF!"

Mal caught up with Rutherford and me. "When I left the North Sea, they were ordering the RAF to airfields near Dover." He said this with hope.

We squinted into the hazed eastern sky, just as the planes peeled off and dove towards us straight out of the sun.

"Stukas and Messerschmitt 109s," Rutherford said, shading his eyes. "Gunners! We need gunners!" he shouted to the ranks up the dunes. He aimed his rifle up at the first Stuka. "Take cover, Colley!"

I paused, unable to turn from the sight. The whistle of the planes swooping down was demonic. Mal frowned. "Hear that?" Mal looked up, catching his breath, his face blotching red. "General Major Wolfram von Richthofen's toy whistles. Bastard! The bombs are equipped with four cardboard whistles, each keyed to a different pitch. Whistles are attached to the planes as well." He grimaced. "They sound like all the devils of hell." Mal raised his rifle. "Colley! Take cover!" As I ran down to the shore, he shouted to the sky, "Rifles are worthless, Rutherford!"

Rutherford yelled, "They've got to dive low. There's still cloud cover to hamper them.

Shoot, man, shoot! At least we're back in the war!"

Whistles attached to bombs screeched; the dunes blew up; sand splattered the air. I threw my body on the wet shore, debris falling around me. I wanted to be with Mum and Dad. I remember praying for real for the first time in my life. "God," I pleaded, "have a look, here. Please help me."

Every Tommy with a rifle shot at the Stukas. Dunes muffled the effect of the bombs, which saved lives. Some bombs hit the water around the lorry-jetty. A few small boats were broken up or had capsized; bodies floated around them. Someone found a Lewis gun and a gunner. A Bren gun appeared without its feet. Gunners rested it on the debris from the beach. Their mates clipped on new barrels as the first smoked hot, and they let go with this new firepower. The last of the planes banked off.

I looked up. Where there had been lines of soldiers, there was a mound of what looked like red jelly. And chunks of flesh and blood were splattered on me. Run! Run! I ran for the lifeboat, frantically splashing water to clean myself. I saw the soldier by the water's edge, still waving and pointing to his legs. I moved on to my boat.

Huddled and shivering from standing in the water, the soldiers milled around the small boats, eager to board. After a few close calls, we steadied my craft and loaded. I had another man on the second oars who had never rowed before. "In and out, in and out, one —two — in and out…" I coaxed. The boat tipped dangerously side to side. I heard another whistle and ducked. The men sat numbly watching me. One of them with a sad, crow-like face said, "Laddie, keep on rowing. When you hear the whistle, the shell's gone by. If you don't hear it, that means it's landed short, or lad, you don't know what hit you."

When we reached *Marie Celine,* she tugged on her anchor. She was surrounded by the scream, splash, and explosion of shells, hundreds of lifeboats, motor launches, and small fishing boats loaded to the gunnels with soldiers, racing for the ships offshore. *Marie Celine's* white hull was smeared with tar and oil and bits of trash. In spite of it all, she still had her grace.

As we came alongside, someone in our boat said, "A real gentleman's boat, she is!" My parents hung over the side helping soldiers up the ladder. Dad's long arms scooped up soldiers as he called, "Come on, you the army! We're not beat yet. Come on lads!"

Though it was unseasonably warm, Dad still wore his formal jacket covered with oilskins, and Mum wore trousers and a checked shirt.

They had given their life jackets to soldiers. They hadn't had time to change clothes or sleep. The previous night we had been out in the Channel with a load of Coldstream Guards and met the destroyer *Javelin*. The soldiers disembarked while *Javelin's* crew lowered cans of petrol, water, bread, Navy cocoa, corned beef, and tea. Some of the stores were to go ashore, but they never got there. Mal, Dad, and I worked the night between runs, cleaning the decks of sand, vomit, oil, mud, blood, spilled food, cigarette butts, and empty packets. Mum worked below replenishing the stew, cleaning and washing up.

The captain of *Javelin* told Dad and Mal that this would be the last day, and that the remainder of the BEF was being evacuated at the Mole at Dunkirk harbour. He said it was going much faster over there.

This last day, I hoisted my human cargo onto the decks of *Marie Celine* and had begun to cast off when I heard Mum call, "Colley! Wait!" Climbing over the men, she disappeared down below and returned with a sandwich of corned beef and mustard and a tin cup of boiled tea. I devoured the food. As she leaned over the rails I saw her, for the first time, with my dad's eyes—a compact, round, beautiful woman, despite the greasy face and wet, dirty hair. Explosions went off and she didn't flinch. I marveled at her powerful arms and strong hands. Suddenly, I remembered the feeling of her holding me in her lap as she let me steer *Marie Celine*. Her hair was curly and silvery and she smelled of lavender. I wanted to kiss her when she bent down to retrieve the cup.

"Mummy!" I wanted to tell her that I was afraid. I wanted to tell her that my ears were buzzing and ringing and that I was having trouble hearing. I wanted to tell her I loved her. I wanted to cry.

She paused, "Colley, are you sure you won't stay here with us? You've done your bit." "I…

She smiled. "I know, Colley."

As I pushed off, the sea erupted with a detonation. The shock wave tossed me away from *Marie*. Smoke and fire rolled over me and ammunition was popping off. Not far from *Marie Celine*, out in the Channel, I could see that one of the Clyde paddle steamers, loaded with soldiers, had been hit and was on fire. Men were jumping off the bow into the oily sea. Lifeboats approached and surrounded the floundering survivors. I checked my parents. They worked on, pulling soldiers up the rope ladders. I hurried to shore for another load. There was nothing to do but keep working.

Throughout that day, most of the BEF were evacuated or marched to the Mole to board the last ships. The Germans had figured out what was happening and didn't want our men coming back to fight them again.

On the beaches, BEF stragglers and French wandered in, some confused, some hysterical, for they were the rearguards and had suffered days of bombing. The ones on stretchers were to wait until the last. Naval officers had arrived in the night with fresh orders from Churchill.

Mal and Rutherford swirled around the soldiers, encouraging some and snapping orders and cursing at others. Mal's uniform, covered with oil and sand, was shredded and ragged. He breathed hard. "Communications are a mess. We just got orders that we must evacuate the French from the Mole. We marched most of the remaining BEF down the beach. Now the French are saying they received orders to wait on the beaches for evacuation!"

Rutherford's face had a blue shadow growth and his eyes looked recessed into two dark holes. "Most of the ships have left. We've just had orders to board the *Malcolm*. Colley, I think this'll be your last trip. Are you ready lad?"

I was dreaming of soft pillows and of sleeping for days, as Mal, Rutherford, and I rowed our last load of French and BEF to *Marie Celine*. When we moved away, I saw more French arriving on the beaches, waiting to board a ship that was not going to come. And I saw the soldier by the water's edge, poor devil, waving his arms and pointing to his legs. New shell craters all around him. I could not take this last load of soldiers without him. I rushed over. Then I saw that he had only one leg. The other had been shot off to a bandaged bloody stump. I ran to the lifeboat and took a line and ran it back to him. I tied it around his rib cage. Then what?

What? I didn't know if I could get him to the water. At that moment, Mal arrived at my side, huffing. "What the fuck!" He looked at me, looked at the amputee, hoisted him up on his shoulders, and waded into the water. With the soldier in tow, Mal swam to *Marie Celine*. Dad, with the help of a few others, pulled their Tommy comrade up by the line.

It was late afternoon by the time we hoisted sail, throttled up, and headed out into the Channel. Dad had to steer through bodies bobbing with the tide, still suspended by life preservers. At times *Marie Celine* stalled in the drifts of our men, as if she were reluctant to leave them behind. "Nothing we can do for them," Dad said, as he patted her deck. "Best get on for the live ones, Old Thing."

There was a break in the bombing. The lifeboats and long boat were fastened in tow, ready to go home. In the distance, from the city of Dunkirk, bombs and heavy detonations roared where the Germans' demolition was proceeding. Our passengers were mostly French, and they appeared sick with fatigue and depression. Mum passed up broth. Our one-legged soldier ate and drank heartily. Mum re-wrapped his bandages. I wondered, would he live through this? Would he make it?

An older infantryman pulled a concertina from his sack. "For our froggies," he said. He played a tune. The mood lightened. Mum passed around bottles of sherry.

I scooted into the cockpit with Mal, Rutherford, and my parents. Mum brought up Dad's Dailuaine single malt. He poured us each a dram and tucked the bottle in a coil of line. Dad had told me that it took the Highland Malt sixteen years to get ready. "It's about twenty now. Older than you, Mal." He held up his glass to us. "All of you did a smashing job." He took a drink and let the flavours linger in his mouth.

I took a sip and let the peaty, smoky richness fill my senses. I watched Mal and Rutherford; each marked surprise as they tasted the rare single-malt whiskey. "Oh Doctor, this is splendid!" Rutherford said. Mal nodded closing his eyes.

"Well, lads, I can't think of a better time to have a dram. We're going home!" He turned to Rutherford. "Rutherford, quite amazing how you got those men organised on the beaches. They were a rough and tumble mob. Some were quite drunk from the French wine cellars, I gather."

"Doctor, do you know my own unit didn't like taking orders from me?" "No. That can't be."

"Oh yes. You see, I was in my first year in Fine Arts at Cambridge when this war came along. I wanted to be a teacher. Simple as that. The men wanted a professional soldier." He looked into his drink and smiled wryly. "Someday I may have the pleasure of seeing some of those bodgies in my classes."

Mal said, "Well, you got them in shape on the beaches." He turned to Dad. "Rutherford had them cleaning the beaches, tidying up."

"Can't let Jerry think we left in a hurry," Rutherford snorted.

"Well said," Mum mused, pursing her lips as she looked over the cargo of weary men.

"Now Mal, lad," Dad said, "are you to be going back to school? Your father was wagering you'd beat Colley to medical school."

Mal blushed. "Doctor, I always wanted to be a career officer. Never told my parents." He took a drink and coughed, his face reddening further. He looked out over the blazing inferno to the west then studied his boots. "I see now what war is really like."

We waited.

Mal raised his eyes and looked around. "We will muddle through… somehow."

Dad said with forced heartiness, "We just get on with it, Mal. We English. That's something Hitler fails to realize. We will win. I'll be in Tahiti with my family. Rutherford, you'll be back at Cambridge teaching young chaps. And reckoning with those bodgies. Mal, you'll be Prime Minister! Thing is, lads, we will not be defeated." He poured us another dram.

We arrived at the *Malcolm* with several other small craft. Crew helped our passengers up to the decks. The captain called Rutherford and Mal to the bridge. I sat in the cockpit with my parents. Dad poured a Scotch for me and Mum. He had been sipping those malts throughout the ordeal. It kept him going and he never nodded or closed an eye once. Mal and Rutherford climbed back down the ship's ladders and joined us. They looked grave.

Dad raised his brows. "Well lads, what is it?"

"Most of the boats have left for Dover. There are French waiting on the beaches." Mal sighed. "They were rearguard for our rearguard. They fought the Germans so our men could make it out. The *Malcolm* can take them, but we need volunteers. We've got a couple of fishing boats...and one sloop."

Mum leaned against Dad's chest. "We'd better go get our French now, before I collapse right here."

Rutherford said, "We'll lower two lifeboats and follow you." Mal and Rutherford climbed back up to the deck and watched us cast off for the last time.

As we pulled away, the enemy aircraft were coming back for their final daytime assault.

This time they were concentrating on the shipping. A steam packet vessel, *Lady Mona*, was standing by to transport French troops, just to port and aft of the *Malcolm*. Bombs exploded around us. We heard a huge crash and saw the steam packet break in half. Her ammunition stores went off, sending rockets and bullets high into the air. Crew and soldiers were struggling in the water, mingling with bodies kept afloat by life belts. Fresh oil was lying thick on the surface, and the men were having trouble getting their heads high enough to breathe.

Dad watched the sky. "Colley, help me watch those aircraft. As soon as one dives, let him come close, then we turn her hard over. It takes them a minute to adjust their course." I took the helm. Dad and I timed the dives and zigzagged, avoiding the fighter planes and bombs as we headed for the victims. *Malcolm*'s crew manned lifeboats. As we neared, soldiers clutched desperately onto our rope ladders. Dad put the engine in neutral. All *Marie Celine*'s sails were up, but they hung limply without wind. The three of us moved to the starboard rail. Our ropes were now slippery with oil, and the men were sliding off.

Stukas dropped from the sky, pulling out of their dives just about mast height. One came for us. I could see the pilot through the transparent cockpit cover. He pulled out and his rear gunner raked us. Bloody holes dotted my parents' backs as Dad slumped over Mum. Not realizing that I was hit, I stumbled for my parents. A detonation rolled *Marie Celine*, and I was thrown into the water. I paddled to get back to the boat where my parents were slumped over the rails. She seemed to be waiting for me, but my legs went numb and I couldn't kick. The currents moved her out of reach. Bombs whistled. Pillars of water raised rolling *Marie* on her starboard side, and I saw my parents slip together into the sea and disappear.

Black smoke and flames slid toward me. *Marie Celine* caught a wisp of wind. Her sails filled and she moved away from me; then she halted, her sails emptied the wind, and she waited for me.

"Colley! Colley?" Mal yelled. He grabbed me by the back of my shirt. Rutherford took my arms, and they pulled me into the lifeboat. I fought. "*Marie Celine*, Mummy, Daddy! She's waiting for us. Let go! *Marie*! I'll come fetch you, *Marie Celine*!"

Mal held me in the boat while Rutherford rowed, between crashing bombs, towards the *Malcolm*. I watched *Marie Celine* shudder, turn slightly, fill her canvas with wind, and ghost away against a world on fire.

FOUR

We the French— Abandoned?

June, 1940 – From the journals of Captain Pierre Jeantot

FROM THE TILE roof of the distillery, I watched Corporal Eric Trubert's motorcycle kick rooster tails of mud and grass as he raced across an open field towards me. Eric was carrying an important letter from my commanding officer, General Blanchard, of the French First Army. A lone Stuka dropped from the sky and followed him, its guns firing. It was out of my rifle range. Eric, a motorcycle racer in our home village, hunched down and did a zigzag pattern. The fighter dove lower, shooting wildly at him, at car-height, then pulled out, looped back and dove again.

Eric hit an irrigation ditch and was thrown from his cycle. The plane headed for him, dove steep, stalled, tried to pull out, and crashed. Eric sat up in the ditch, as the plane exploded into flames.

I ran downstairs to the main tank rooms yelling, "Louis, cover me!"

Resting against the stairwell, Louis jumped up and held his rifle as if it were a burning ember. It was nearly as tall as his bony, adolescent frame. Blowing threads of yellow hair from his eyes, he fumbled with the trigger device, "I am only the cook, Capitaine. I am frightened."

"Private Mourier, at this moment we have no food. You are unable to cook. You must learn to shoot."

Louis nodded and looked at the gun, unsure, "Yes…I want to shoot."

"Paco, come here!" I called out, my voice higher than I wanted.

Sergeant Paco Torres filled the front entrance. Weathered, short, and plump, he was a fierce fighter.

"Cover me, Paco. I will get Eric."

When I reached Eric, he was smoking a cigarette and watching the Stuka burn.

"Eric! Are you hurt?"

"No, Pierre, *mon capitaine*, I am not yet dead!" he said this with forced heartiness.

"I see. Then Corporal, how dare you endanger your life and the life of your commanding officer. We are targets in this open space!" I realized he was quaking violently. He grinned and aimed the butt of the cigarette for his mouth and missed. He did not seem to notice.

"Come, we must get back under cover." I pulled him up. He looked anxiously at his motorbike. "Do not worry, Eric. Paco will retrieve your bike after dark." I slipped his pouch over my shoulder, hooked my arm in his, and pulled him across the field.

Gun thunder shook the ground. The edges of the world around us were stained with spots of smoke. Von Bock's tanks rumbled closer. They had reached the coast at Nieuport. The afternoon was hot and sticky, but I could hear Eric's teeth clacking.

I sat with my company on the raised platforms that held oak upright brandy *foudres*. Awkwardly, Louis held Eric in the crook of his skinny arm. It seemed incongruous, Louis the child, holding Eric, our village's handsome boy-hero of motorcycle racing. Paco smoked, brooded, and stared out the windows over the grey flatlands. This land was colourless compared to the rich buckskin hills, azure seas, and cadmium reds of our home, Valras, in Provence. The wounded Englishman, Rod, slept nearby.

Our headquarters, this main tank room in a distillery in Belgium, somewhere near the border of France, was damp and cool. The sharp tang of alcohol, mixed with toasted wood, misted around us. Water trickled in troughs and drains that ran along the brick floors. Glass beakers, hoses, pumps, and barrel tools were abandoned on workbenches. Opening the valves of one of the uprights, I poured us each a beaker of the young brandy. That was all the nourishment we had, brandy and cigarettes. It did not take long for Eric to stabilize. I opened the message.

The dispatch was dated Friday, May 31, 1940. Today was Monday, June 3, late afternoon. I hesitated, not sure I could believe what the message said. It was much worse than we could have possibly imagined.

I looked at what remained of my company. Paco Torres, an apprentice in my father's boatyard; his father worked for mine. Eric Trubert, a farmer's son and motorcycle racer, lived in the delta, near my family's house. Louis Mourier worked with his family in their bistro in my village. He had run away from our home village to join us. Until now, we had been able to keep him safe. Our wounded Englishman Rod, slept fitfully. It had become increasingly difficult for him to walk. In such a short time, the world had changed and we might easily die here, far from our homes. How would I tell them?

I thought back on the last few days.

When King Leopold surrendered on May 28th, my company and I were trapped in Flanders—a land that reminded me of dreary food counters of leek soup, with small nickel ridges holding the grey-green liquid within the chafing dishes. The ridges were roads, high roads that ran along dikes and irrigation ditches, connecting farms, towns, and villages, all with high-pitched roofs of red tile. Clusters of thin, black-green trees slit the murky sky. My company had been cut off from the brigade, the brigade from the division. I was left in command of a remaining company of twenty men, most of them from my region of Languedoc. Our weapons were World War One vintage, and we had only ten rifles among us with a few rounds each, one heavy artillery gun, a roll of detonation wire, one motorcycle, and a horse-drawn wood-burning camp stove. I was a captain. There were no other commanding officers about. Our last orders from command headquarters were to defend France to the last man, to hold back the Germans, and to establish a bridgehead around Dunkirk. We hoped to re-unite with our division.

The high roads were clotted with Belgian troops, tanks, lorries, staff cars, dead horses, cattle, and frantic refugees shouting and crying. Convoy horns honked until the sound became one bleat. We could make no headway forward. The poor were piled in wheelbarrows, clutching bundles, blankets draped over their shoulders. Refugees escaped on bicycles, on foot, on hay carts pulled by the strongest children, and in milk carts pulled by dogs. Mattresses were stacked on the makeshift vehicles, the only protection from diving fighter planes. A staff car with Belgian officers inched past us. Down the road, I saw the officers climb out, change into civilian clothes and disappear into the crowd. We snatched up their deserted rifles and ammunition.

Roadblocks backed up all traffic for as far as fifteen kilometers, and delays were hours. We managed to get our gear down one of the irrigation ditches; then we marched over the spongy, light green of the lowlands for the Dunkirk bridgehead.

A long canal between Furnes and Bergues marked the outermost periphery of the Dunkirk bridgehead. We were told that part of our division would be holding off the Germans at Furnes, on the south of the canal. The British would be holding the north end of the canal, closest to Dunkirk. We crept along the shady, poplar-lined north side of the canal towpath just outside of the red brick village of Furnes. The area was deserted. No English. No French. No Germans. The guns had stopped. The silence was frightening. The silence between battles.

As we reached the edge of the village I halted and said, "I need a scout." Though the men were exhausted and anxious, all twenty stepped forward. I picked Marc, a sturdy young private, and Paco, for they appeared to be the most alert. Marc and Paco took the lead. My company and I followed shortly after.

As soon as we moved around the bend, rifle fire snapped and whistled from one of the houses. I saw Marc had fallen, wounded. Paco was surrounded by English soldiers. Before we could take cover, we were surrounded. We dropped our guns and raised our hands in the air.

"We are French!" I said in English. "French Company…"

I heard the clicks as they cocked their rifles and fell silent. They were nervous, snarling.

A sergeant came forward, training his pistol on me. The hammer snicked. He was a rough-looking sort. And he was wet with sweat. This soldier could go off any moment and I knew that. "Your English is far too good for a Frenchman. We just shot ten Jerry dressed up as French soldiers!" He was as young as we were. But he was fresher and full of fire.

"I apprenticed in England."

"Where?"

"Southampton"

He seemed to turn this over in his mind a second. "And what's in Southampton?"

"Boats. I build boats." I had to mentally translate into English. My words were studied, precise.

"Southampton's known for boatyards, Captain. What else can you tell me?"

"My father, he is a boatbuilder in Southern France. I was sent to work at Camper and Nicholson as an apprentice in naval architecture and boat construction. I lived with an English family, the Camper family."

"What sort of boats?"

"Pleasure yachts."

"Name one of their yachts."

"*Angela.*" My mind raced. I hoped that was the right name.

The sergeant raised his spiky brows. He challenged, "I know boats. My uncle and father worked in that yard." I knew then that my life was on the line, more than ever. I told him what I knew of the particulars of this yacht. He listened intently. He furrowed his brows, "Wrong, Captain." I stiffened for the blow. He snapped, "Launched '34."

I tilted my head in acquiescence. "I may have been mistaken. I was quite young then." He shifted, averting his head slightly, but his eyes

never left me. After a moment of this, he waved his gun. "As you were."
The English soldiers relaxed, but kept a wary watch on my unit. After
a moment of hesitation, my men lowered their hands.

"What are you doing here?" he asked me.

"We have come to help. I am Capitaine Pierre Jeantot. This is what
is left of my unit."

"Oh, you've come to help? Or have you run away like the rest of
your lot?" He pointed his gun towards the village. "Like the rest of the
deserters, I'll wager you want food. We have no fucking food to spare."

This was unbearable. I did not know if my men understood, but
they sensed the tone; they closed up behind me.

I maintained calm. By the collective mood of our men, any slip
could erupt into violence.

I said, "We were ordered to fall back and meet our unit here. We
were ordered to establish a bridgehead with the British. We marched
here, with many casualties along the way. We did not run. And for your
information we have a French chef. And we have…food." This last bit,
the food bit, was an exaggeration, I confess.

He said, "We were ordered to meet the French and establish a
bridgehead. No bloody French. No bloody English. Nothing here but
dead bastards." He shook his head, rubbed his chin and grimaced.
"Help us?" he repeated to himself. He surveyed my dazed, beaten group
of men, and let out a long sigh. "Captain…sorry I popped off like that.
We are fagged." He held out his hand, "Sergeant Rod Slater." I shook
his hand. We saluted. Both companies snapped up, looked sharp, and
fell into a formation of sorts, as if life were back to normal, and we
were safely on a parade ground in London or France…young boys in
school again, as we should have been at this time of our lives. Paco supported our wounded Marc.

"Carry on, Captain." He said this with brittle resolve.

We fell in with the English and, in silence, marched up the road.

The village had been hit hard. Corpses of German, French, and English soldiers, civilians, refugees, horses, cats, and dogs littered the streets.

Flies were thick. The warm, heavy air smelled of rotting flesh, cordite, and smoke. Most of the buildings had been shelled. Every street was filled with smashed glass, broken brick, and splintered furniture. Ditched tanks, lorries, and artillery were phantom images through the smoke of small fires. Sniper fire came from a house across the canal. We disbanded and fled from structure to structure.

Finally, at the headquarters in the village square, in a cellar in the bombed-out government house, we settled in. The English soldiers attempted to speak French; the French attempted first-level English. Water was available from the courtyard garden fountain. After a time of milling around and looking towards us with anticipation, Sergeant Slater gave his men a nod. The English went deeper into the cellar and came back with food. They had scavenged potatoes, bottled asparagus, bottled chicken, cabbages, onions, wine, and beer from different root cellars abandoned in the town. Louis turned the horse out into the garden. Along the way he had found leeks, onions, chervil, and potatoes. Under cover of the high brick walls, he stoked the camp stove and did what he was born to do: cook. The men ate fiercely.

Sergeant Slater and I sat off to the side. He poured red wine into my cup and told me he had been with the Durham Light Infantry and that most of his division had been lost in the retreat from Arras. "I was the only officer left with a few men. On retreat, we bumped into these units of odds and ends. All of us were under the same orders. We were told to defend the retreat line, at Furnes. My company's an assortment of lost details. I've got machine gunners to communications men, field surveyors to anti-tank gunners. There're only fifty of us now. We've got one anti-tank rifle with one magazine of 160 rounds, two lorries, a few Brens, and a Lewis.

When we got to this village, we marched into a nest of advancing Jerry. The BEF wasn't here. No bloody ammo, no bloody reinforcements. Bloody hell."

He went on to say that he and his men had been exchanging fire with the enemy, holding them off across the canal.

Sergeant Slater sopped up Louis's stew with a piece of hard bread.

He wiped his mouth on a dirty sleeve, took a long pull on his wine, and lit a cigarette. "Smoke, Captain?"

I took the cigarette with relish. "You realize it is the same with us. So different were our expectations. We marched into this land of Belgique. Ah, it was beautiful! The villagers ran to us with flowers, chickens, milk, cheese. The girls kissed us. Then on our retreat, the villages were deserted. Only Louis, who is a child, said, 'Capitaine, how is it that all these Belgique are making the laundry today?' I had to tell him. The white sheets hanging from windows, fences, barns, and rooftops were the flags of surrender. We were allowed no food when we asked. The villagers took the pump handles from the water fountains. We were allowed no water!"

Slater flicked at the embers of his cigarette. "It was the same with us. Captain, I haven't told my men, but I'm afraid our army has gone for good. And the brass doesn't know we're here. Our orders were to hold off Jerry…to the last man. We were supposed to get reinforcements, ammunition. We're left; that's what I think. Forgotten!"

"So, it is the same. We were told to come here and hold the line with you."

"Jerry is about a mile from here, in the trees. Tanks. They've built a pontoon bridge over the canal." He laughed dryly, "Captain, it looks bloody hopeless." He looked into his cup.

A shell hit above. A sentry scrambled down the stairs, "Tanks! Up the road!"

By the time we took up our positions along the entrance to the village, two of the English outer guns had destroyed a number of enemy vehicles and a few tanks as they advanced towards us. But the German tanks stampeded down the road, trampling everything in sight. It was over in less than thirty minutes.

Slater and I gave orders to the few men left to retreat to headquarters. As we skipped from building to building, nearing the headquarters, a shell hit the garden, knocking out the fountain and part of the wall. We crawled back behind the ruins and into the cellar. Louis, the child for whom I was responsible, was not there. I crept back to the garden. The cook stove was a twisted, smouldering mass of metal. Frantic, I waded through the high foliage and grass. I heard Louis's small voice soothing. He was kneeling over the horse, trying to close the horse's eyes.

His hands passed over the lids and still the horse stared up at him. I tried to pull him away. "No!" he sobbed, frantically covering the horse's eyes with his hands.

"Louis, eyes of the dead, they do not stay closed."

He pulled away from me. "No! I cannot leave him like this!" He was out of his mind. I had to think fast. He wore only his uniform shirt. I had a field jacket. I took it off and tucked it around the forehead of the horse and under his cheeks. Louis patted the hooded face of the horse and let me lead him to the cellar.

The Germans quieted down. Slater and I sent the wounded off ahead in the last lorries.

No room for us. There were five of us left: Paco, Louis, Eric, Sergeant Rod Slater, and I, Capitaine Pierre Jeantot, leader of the last of the French army. We had rifles, very little ammunition, some bottles of wine, a few jugs of water, and cases of English cigarettes.

"You know, Captain, we're surrounded. I don't know about you, but I'm not about to be captured."

"We are with you, Sergeant."

"They're pushing us to the beaches. That's the only way out of here."

It was then I noticed Slater was bleeding from his hip. He had stuffed a rag into his pants in the front. The knee was bloody as well.

"Let us have a look, Sergeant."

"Damned if it didn't go right through to my knee, Captain. I swear, I don't feel a fucking thing. I can march just fine."

The bullet had gone through his left hip and out through the knee. If there were pieces of shrapnel, we could not see them. I cleaned the wound the best I could without field dressing.

Louis came to my side. "I found this, Capitaine." He pulled a small jar of honey from under his shirt. I puzzled, thinking he had finally lost his mind. "There is not enough for the men."

He offered, "Let me attend that wound."

"Louis, are you sure?"

"Yes, sir. My grandmother healed wounds. Cleaned them with honey. It keeps the germs away." Louis cleaned the wound with a maternal gentleness. He removed the coagulated blood, and once he had coated it with honey, he wrapped wine-soaked rags around the wound.

I said, "Louis, you should be a physician. I see that you have a talent."

Sergeant Slater raised his head, "Captain, if you don't mind, am I right?"

I took a good look. "Yes, Sergeant, the bullet missed the important parts of you."

"Thank you, Captain."

Under cover of night we skulked through small woods and swampy terrain. We could hear Germans and see their forms in the mists curling off the river. We took our only communication with the outside world: a motorbike. Supporting Slater in turn, we retreated through the night to this distillery, from where I sent Eric off with a dispatch and requests for orders—the orders that I was about to report to my group.

Slater groaned from his palette of a woolen great coat and rose up on his elbow. "Hey, you frogs. How's a bloke to get a smoke around here?" He rose stiffly and limped over to our group. Paco gave him a smoke and a cup of brandy. Slater took a long draught and made a face. "What's this? Piss?"

Louis answered in his best waiter's fashion, "This, Sergeant, this is Eau-de-Vie-de-Marc." Holding up his cup and inspecting the tin as if seeing a fine wine through the battered metal, he said, "A brandy made from the remains of fermentation: seeds, pulp, skins…not consumed so much in our part of France. However, it can be pleasant." He took a sip.

Slater swallowed hard and shook it off. "I'll have another!"

They huddled around me. I lit a cigarette and blew out the smoke. "In general, our communications have completely collapsed. As you know, being trapped in Flanders, we were cut off from main headquarters. We only had the wireless, which ended up to be via our Navy, and their headquarters at Maintenon, far from Paris. They ordered us to defend the French flag. The orders to evacuate with the English to the beaches never reached us."

"*Merde!*" Eric spat.

"Shit, shit, shit!" Slater pushed smoke out between his clenched teeth.

Louis blinked at Paco. Paco's mouth twisted downward; he gave Louis a defiant shrug.

I continued. "It was decided that we French must be evacuated to England—'rescued,' it said, 'to fight again another day.' Our forces could not get enough ships to take us off the beaches. There are English ships waiting to sail us to England. They are there, now, at Bray-Dunes, not far from Dunkirk. Prepare to march." I looked over my men: shell-shocked, after days without sleep and no food except that short bit of nourishment back in Furnes before the shelling started. I was afraid they would not be able to move. In their eyes was the stare of passive resignation.

With a few canteens of slimy cistern water from the distillery, flasks of the young, rough marc, and cartons of English cigarettes we made off at dusk. Eric, with regret, destroyed the motorcycle. We hooked our fingers in the belts of the man ahead. The leader stayed awake and marched for the beach. In half-hour turns, each of us supported Slater. This way we could walk in our sleep.

Included in the last dispatch was a map from a French travel bureau, naming hotels, fine dining establishments, and vacation spots on the beaches. That was a long time ago. But it was not hopeless. We knew the way. The way was marked by the cumulous towers of smoke in the sky, tinged with luminescent, lava-red. The end of the road. The end of the world. Backed to the sea by the enemy.

Across fields and woods we moved, hiding when we saw silhouettes of tanks and soldiers against a raging sky. We passed outside the Belgian sea resort of La Panne. It was festooned with burning incendiaries, like candles on a cake. Fire vomited from the roofs of houses. Gunfire rattled the ground. Skirting the towns, we reached the beaches at midnight.

We crested the dunes at the edge of the sloping beaches. Enemy flares lit a paralyzing sight. Platinum bellies of bombers flashed over the Channel, as they dropped flares. Mercurial shapes of destroyers flicked on and off against the horizon, flames blowing out of their guns. Planes screamed and wheeled. Guns thudded from the ships, ten rounds a minute.

What lay before us was more horrible.

Louis, struggling with Slater, shuffled up beside me. Slater leaned on us both, peering down at the beach, "Christ, they've all gone."

Louis's falsetto voice cracked with indignation. "There is no one. No boats."

Paco and Eric stepped up. Eric said, "It is over. We are dead. There is no way out."

Paco said, "The English have left us. If I live, I will never forgive the dirty English!" Paco's sunken black eyes glistened, reflecting the red clouds and falls of fire going off in the Channel.

Slater said, "Mate, if they're not here for us, there's a damn good reason."

"Ships can yet come," I said. "They cannot reach us now. It is obvious the Germans are concentrating on the vessels in the Channel. Wait until morning. There is nothing we can see. It is too dark. We will dig a small trench here in the dune and rest. Who takes first watch?"

When I got into the trench I did not care what happened. Already my company of starved, weak men had fallen asleep. I knew no one was going to take watch. I confess I did not care about anything— shellfire booming, shaking the sand below me, the approaching enemy, the war—I wanted never to wake up. I knew in the morning the ships would not be there and we would either be shot or taken prisoner by the Germans. I passed into sleep. I had to sleep. Sleep.

The quiet woke us. A cloud cover had padded in during the predawn. Enemy planes had gone. There were no ships on the horizon. Silence rang. The Channel was streaks of silver-grey silk meeting a velvety, grey-pink sky. The tide was out. Dawn moved like a slow-rolling wave across the beach below. Light washed over abandoned overcoats, Lewis and Bren guns, empty crates, cable, ropes, tins and wine bottles, rucksacks, kit bags, torched and twisted lorries, burned-out ambulances, vehicles piled into jetties that reached out into the Channel waters, and the corpses of those left behind. *So*, I thought, *this is what we have come to. This is the end of France. The end of the civilized world. Tomorrow we all start speaking German.*

With mounting despair, we followed dawn's beam as if it were the last lighthouse on earth, across the ruins to the sea, over piles of wrecked, sunken boats. It swept out and spotlighted a sailboat—an intact sailboat, bobbing slightly on her side, up on a shoal. Loose sheets coiled in the air and rapped against the spars. Her sails lifted lazily and fell like great wings. A dream, I thought. But the others saw it too. I said, "We go."

Eric threw Slater over his shoulders, and we ran down the beach and waded out. The last deepest part of the way we swam and floated Slater on a piece of debris until we grabbed the boarding ladders hanging off her sides. We reached the decks and checked for signs of life, or enemy. The boat was deserted. We rolled on our backs, puffing from the minor exertion. Our backs stuck to coagulated blood, sand, teak slivers, vomit, and butts of cigarettes. Louis sat up and looked around. "An angel. An angel ship has saved us."

"Not until we can get her off this sandy shoal and running," I said. We had to move quickly.

Armed with Slater's pistol, I ventured down the companionway. Before me was a chateau, veiled by the necessities of war. Sand and oil marred the teak cabin sole; kit bags, crushed packets of cigarettes, tin plates and cups cluttered the floor. There were bandages, medicine bags, water and food, coal, lockers of clothes, blankets—enough to last us months. The dank must of unwashed men, oil, and filthy sea-soaked uniforms steamed in the closed air. I opened the scuppers. Light and sea mist filtered inside. I put Louis in charge of food and rationed out a small amount of bread for energy until we could get the boat underway. Louis properly bandaged Slater. He was able to find morphia in the medicine bag. Louis held up a syringe. "I have helped my father with the animals. I think I can do it." With a special finesse, Louis was able to plunge the needle in the proper place and successfully sedate Slater. We bunked him up forward, in a small stateroom.

We had to escape before the cloud cover lifted. Paco removed the rope ladders from the boat's hull. She showed herself more like a proper yacht, however filthy and shot-up. Eric and I got into the engine house and discovered that the diesel engine was in good condition; it had simply run out of fuel. There were cans of fuel lashed to the decks.

I looked at the hoses, intakes, fan belts, exhaust, and I wondered, was this engine harmed in any way? It looked new. No rust. No dirt! I said, "Eric, I knew you would be good for something. Can you make her run?" Eric became fused with a new energy, as he checked oil, opened and closed sea-cocks, tapped on the heads, heat exchanger, and transmission. "*Mon capitaine*, this is a jewel of an engine! It was in neutral when it ran aground. Propeller is free. The transmission should be good. I can make this engine run!"

The thick teak-planked decks were rent and splintered with bullet holes, but intact. The front of the forward cabin was damaged in places. The boat's documentation numbers had been carved in the interior. We would have to cover those numbers somehow. On the whole, this angel was sound throughout. The seams were tight, her rigging was in perfect shape, and there were extra sails, lines, and tools below.

The tide began to change. "Paco, we have to get her off the sand!" I ran from one side of the boat to the other. The lead keel was cut deep into the sand. "Eric! Louis!"

Paco appeared at my side and glimpsed over the rails. "I am not used to a keel this deep. This boat is heavy. Deep draft." He looked up the masts and down to the sails. Resisting, he said, "I am not accustomed to sails like this."

"Paco, pay attention. All boats are the same! This is simply a new boat. I feel a wind is coming!" I was frantic. I had to figure this boat's systems. I followed the mainsheet to its winch and to the cleats. I un-cleated the sheet and pulled on the winch; its ratcheting sound echoed off the fog. Slowly, with each turn of the winch, the heavy boom moved inboard and lifted with the new strength of a tightened mainsail that seemed to breathe slightly in the breeze. The foresail sheets had been led back through blocks to the cockpit. Wrapping them on the winch, I took a few turns. The foresail caught some wind, enough to shudder the boat. Paco glared at the sails, disbelieving. "Paco," I ordered, angry with his balking, "trace the sheets for the other sails and get them set." Deliberately slow, Paco searched for the lines needed.

Louis and Eric came on deck. We rocked it, first standing on the port rails then running to the starboard, shifting the weight. Nothing happened. This boat's lead keel was firmly in the sand. Coiling line, Paco sneered. "This is a devil boat. We will be shot here, like ducks."

Eric, Louis, and I all stopped and stared at him. "Has this war made you crazy, Paco?" I yelled. "I am your captain. Cleat that line and help us. Now! Or you will be arrested when we get home." He sauntered over and threw his weight into rocking the boat. Beyond the cloud cover, we heard the faint hum of aircraft. Fear shot through me. This was our last hope, this ship. If we waited for high tide, we would be caught, or shot. She had to move. Move now. For a second, I squeezed my eyes shut and prayed to Jesus, Mary, and Joseph. I also gave a quick plead to St. Jude the Impossible. The aircraft was droning louder.

After a pause, light air filled the sails; they fluttered and heaved. The four of us put our backs to the main boom and pushed it outboard of the high side of the boat. "Jesus, Mary, and Joseph," I whispered. Wind hit the mainsail with a thump. The hull moved and rocked over to right itself. We cheered. Paco looked at the sails, astonished. The boat lifted, floated, and moved away from the beaches. We had a wind freshening; the water sucked and gurgled around the hull.

Eric jumped below and started up the engine. It purred. I got to the helm. I felt we were under the protection of something beyond this world...an angel ship.

At that moment, the guns started up on the English side of the Channel. Our side was quiet. There was still a heavy cloud cover. We passed the beaches, rocking slightly in the swell. The wind was easterly, remarkable for that time of year. We headed away from the shore and let out the sails. The tide bucked us a bit, but we had a strong engine. I remember thinking, could it be that we are saved? The thunder of the guns rattled through the hull. Still, we were alone for the moment, hidden under the pall of black smoke that was Dunkirk. The wind was carrying us out the English Channel to the sea outside. The wind also carried the black smoke with us like the cloak of God. It was a miracle.

Eric and Paco came into the cockpit. I worried, "We cannot go to England. The battle is concentrated across our path. They would gun us down."

"What can we do? This is horrible." Eric was trying to light a cigarette in the wind. Paco drew hard on his smoke, ignoring his mate's need for a light. "Damn the English," he said. "Damn them."

I flipped through some charts retrieved from the chart table. I unrolled flags discovered in the flag locker. It all seemed to fall into place. I said, "We change clothes, get out fishing gear, destroy our papers and any boat papers, fly the Spanish flag, speak Spanish, and head this angel ship home, to Valras."

"What about Sergeant Slater, that English?" Paco asked.

"He will never fight again. He will have to learn French. He will live in France until he gets well, then, it is our duty to get him home. Paco take the helm, while I figure this course."

I went below. The coal stove had been stoked, and it was feverishly hot. A pinafore printed with spring flowers covered Louis's filthy, tattered uniform. He looked natural in the galley, like a French woman in her kitchen. A cigarette dangled from his mouth as he hovered over a pot of foul-smelling stew.

The chart table was in an alcove with a bench seat and a table with a lid that lifted. Pilot charts, plotting charts, and navigation tools were within. A bronze chronometer nestled in its wooden box on a fiddled shelf. Sailing directions, navigation books, and a wireless were stowed on the bulkhead shelves. The ship's papers and nameplate were under the chart table. The bronze nameplate gave the ship's name, *Marie Ce-*

line, the builder, Dr. Richard Neville, the boatyard, Philip and Son, Dartmouth, Devon. I burned all the ship's papers in the coal stove. Then I detached the nameplate and went forward to the small stateroom in which we had bunked Slater. Drowsy, he was looking through the contents of a small brass box sitting on his chest. "Where did you get that?" I said.

His eyes half closed, he slurred, "Found this in the mattress. Hurt my backside. Have a look at these." He fanned out the deck of dirty French cards.

"Never mind that. This is perfect," I said, putting the nameplate in the box and gathering the decks of girly cards from Slater's chest and returning them as well. He leaned over on his side and pulled the mattress back. "There's a hidden door in the bunk platform. See it?"

I found the little trap door, hid the box and replaced the trap door. Looking over the wood, I really would not find this door unless someone pointed it out to me. "Perfect," I said again. But Slater was sleeping. I went topsides and told the crew about my discovery.

The smoke from the oil tanks of Dunkirk thickened; we covered our noses and mouths.

Our eyes stung. Under the shroud of black oil smoke, there was no sun, no life. Corpses, cork lifejackets, tin helmets, jagged timbers of ships covered with the shiny, thick sludge floated by us. The easterly wind freshened, pushing us on a confused sea, away from hell.

FIVE

Translated Logbook and Journals of Pierre Jeantot

June 16, 1940. Log entries.

*S*OMEWHERE NEAR THE Bay of Biscay. We are blown off course. Heavy gale. Confused seas.

The German gunboat can be seen from the tops of waves. He disappears when we are in the troughs. For aching seconds, we see nothing but confused seas churning and colliding from all directions. It is a game of hide and seek. We slide and crash into the bottom of a trough. The gunboat, his rocket-shaped bow peaks over the ridge of a wave and falls back down. We climb, reach the top of a crest, but he is gone. We see nothing but seething valleys of grey foam-streaked seas. And in a flash of silver, he appears again.

What can we do? The engine has stopped. Yesterday we ripped our smaller foresail. Only a storm-sail is up, like a tiny triangular flag, keeping us moving. The noise is shattering our nerves. Sail popping, full, fitful. Snapping and cracking when wind is dumped. We fight at the helm to keep this boat from broaching and coming up abeam to the waves. Crouching low in the cockpit, fighting the runaway helm, we tether ourselves to the boat to keep the waves from sucking us out and overboard. Too rough to cook.

Rotten food is strewn over the galley. We are tired, seasick, and soaked from watches at the helm. We have developed saltwater boils (except Slater, who is confined to a drier bunk). Paco is at the helm. Louis is wedged in the companionway watching for the gunboat. Eric is braced against the doorway of the engine room, cleaning fuel filters and cursing.

I am standing (for it is too painful to sit on these boils), wedged in the chartroom, to say in this log, that the gunboat, he is closing in on us. There is no escape. I look around this marvelous yacht, and I feel an irrational sense that somehow this angel will not let us down. This angel has a spirit that is strong beyond our human doubts and frailty.

* * * *

June 16. From the journals of Captain Pierre Jeantot.

A short time later, we heard the warning shots from the German boat. Flying off a wave, he nearly rammed us. Crew in black foul-weather gear struggled to keep balanced on the heaving deck. A loud hailer screeched at us in German. Paco and I were holding the helm hard over to keep from broaching. We knew no German. Frantically, we shook our heads warning them off as our boat slid sideways down the face of a wave into a trough. At the bottom of this valley of water, *Marie* quivered and stalled. The gunboat teetered on the wave above us. I saw his bottom paint, his chine, his keel. They attempted to fall in beside us. *Marie* was low profile, deep in the water, with little freeboard and a low cabin. One of the crew holding a hawser, poised himself on the gunboat's bow to jump onto our deck. If he got aboard and secured us to their boat, we would certainly be discovered, and Slater could not pass for anything other than English. I made the sign of the cross and prayed.

Again, the German boat opened his engines and sped up beside us. The crewman once more prepared to leap. Our mysterious *Marie* yawed, yanking the helm from our grips. We held on helplessly while the storm-sail filled with wind and took *Marie* up the backside of a wave, then hurled her, surfing down the other side, away from the gunboat. The German boat was caught by a freak wave and shot up into the air high above us. We saw his propeller leave the water and stop. The gunboat landed hard, knocking the gun turrets askew. We could see he was dead in the water, wallowing helplessly as waves from all directions washed over and battered him about.

I heard our own engine start up. Eric poked his head out the hatch, "Full speed ahead, *mon capitaine*!"

At that moment the wind died and started up stronger from the shore, blowing us out of the dangerous trap of the Bay of Biscay and setting the crippled gunboat far offshore. Incredible that the wind blew from the shore this time of year. More profoundly I felt this little angel of a boat had magic. We were Blessed! Blessed! We had escaped and soon would be home, through the Straits of Gibraltar and up into the Golfe Du Lion. Home to our village, Valras.

* * * *

We arrived at our home port malnourished, covered with boils, and suffering from the beginnings of scurvy. Louis, Eric, and Paco were taken home and nursed by their families. Slater was hidden in the attic rooms of my family house. Dr. Mourier tended to us. We slept and we slept. One morning my father woke me. He looked toil-worn. His thick, dark hair fell uncombed on each side of his hollow-cheeked face.

Father said, "Son, the English, he is recovering. We must get him out of here! If we are found with an English, we will be shot. We are now fighting in the war to free France. This war is far more dangerous."

I remember thinking that my father had fought in the last war. He did not have to fight this war—this war that I and my comrades had just survived. Had we lost France?

He spoke in a scatty manner, "Son, our Third Republic gone in disgrace. Surrender! We do not accept surrender! Prime minister Reynaud resigned. The Germans marched in. Marshal Petain, you know the old World War One hero? He is a puppet for the Nazis. He, that old man, he let the Nazis run over Paris while he set up a government in Vichy! Traitor!"

It took me a moment to comprehend this. I was still weak. Before me was a man who was normally well-appointed, in starched shirts, slicked hair, and a face so clean-shaven he had razor burn. Now he was in a dirty peasant shirt and my grandfather's old braces holding up a filthy pair of work pants. A holstered pistol was slung over his shoulder. I was disturbed.

My father's eyes were burning with intensity. He clenched my shoulders and his voice rose to a high, quivery pitch. "There is a savior! A junior general. Charles de Gaulle. He did not accept the surrender. He wants we who agree with him to join him in fighting on. We are fighting to win our country back. We are the Free French. We will get the Germans out of our country.

"But my son, there are other factions against us. Communists, Royalists, the Vichy collaborators. We can trust no one. Before someone finds that we have your English, we must get him back to England. Now."

* * * *

Slater and I were sent to a Free French safe house. We were seven people crowded around a small table in the smoke-filled kitchen of Madame Cormeau, widow, and her fourteen-year-old daughter, Jeanine. The three men with us were Free French Resistance fighters. The heavy, dark curtains were closed. A small lantern lit the room. The group was arguing among themselves.

Madame Cormeau's eyes were mere clefts in the deep folds of her skin. A kerchief woven in colours of yellow, azure blue, ochre, and violet—the colours of Provence—was wound tightly around her head. Her hardy voice dominant, she led the group.

"We cannot carry him over the Pyrenees. He would never make it. Regard you, this man is not able to walk in a normal fashion. First, we would have to get him to the safe house in Perpignan. To get him there, we would use the trains. We cannot take him on the train. Much too dangerous. We would be shot because of the Englishman." Madame sniffed and crossed her arms.

Slater huffed and spoke in the worst French, "*Je pense que je comprend de…*"

Madame threw up her hands in exasperation to the group. "You see? He cannot be interrogated. Even if we get him on the train to Perpignan, or better, to the Carcassonne-Quillan-Pyrenees route, he must understand his briefings on what to say if caught. Briefings on when and where he will change over couriers, or guides. He must understand them. Impossible!" She grimaced at Slater.

Slater leaned close to me and said under his breath, "Captain, did you ever see such a hard woman?"

I raised my brows. "Yes," I whispered. "She has had a hard life. Her husband was killed early in the war. She is a good woman, with the most beautiful daughter in the village."

Slater smiled, "Yes, that's some girl, Captain, some girl."

Jeanine moved into the lantern light and set a fresh *pichet* of red wine before us. Coarse strands of her long, loose hair glistened chestnut and gold. Her round face was cream-white, with wide-set chestnut eyes that flickered to the rafters, around the table, and rested on Slater.

One of the men, called Guy, a young, fair man with a Parisian accent, spoke. "We must get him out by sea. Feluccas. Such a numerous and common boat in the Mediterranean Sea, no one would notice. The problem is to get him from the beach out to the felucca, which will get him to the merchant ship and home." He looked at me. "An innocent day on one's yacht. Yes? Pierre? A little fishing, drinking, picnic for your friends? And we slip a passenger on to the felucca."

Madame nodded, approving, impressed. She turned to Slater and scoffed, "And you English, gone. Never to return. We French will be left to fight this war."

"I'll return, Madame. We'll win this war together." He smiled bravely at Madame Cormeau, but his eyes were on the lovely Jeanine. Madame poofed out her cheeks, gave a shrug, and lit a cigarette.

I and my old crew, Eric and Louis and Slater, cleaned up our angel boat as best we could to make her appear as a yacht once again. Paco disappeared. To Spain, perhaps? We were too busy to bother. On the appointed night, my father arrived with Slater craftily dressed as a Frenchman. Dirty-white peasant shirt, black trousers, and a beret.

German occupation of the Mediterranean Coast of France was not yet an organized danger. In the black of night, we met the felucca offshore about seven kilometers. I helped Slater aboard the tossing boat and into the hands of a crew of Polish seaman and French Resistance fighters. "I'll be back, Captain," he yelled against the crash of the sea. I waved. He did not see my tears.

That is how it began. We became part of the Free French Resistance. The key to our success in saving thousands of lives was our enchanted angel boat, *Marie Celine*.

SIX

Elizabeth Whitehead
Reflects

May 1940

*M*OVING TO THE country was dreadfully boring. Nothing happened. Mummy and I had to stay with Gram at her farm near Deal. We had to leave London because of bombs. Dad was away. He was a medical officer, working on a ship in a secret place. I was to go to a dull, old school. Nobody seemed to care about appearances round here. The styles were so old-fashioned. No cinema. No parties. No dances. Fancy! I spent my time dreaming of going back and seeing my friends. But all my friends were moved out to the country as well. Really, I didn't know where everybody went. Anyway, the first week at Gram's I hid beneath the bed and would not come out.

But one day in June, something happened. I was so happy because Mum and I had to travel to Ramsgate. I wore my best frock. Mum, of course, wore one of her tweed skirts, a jumper, and those brown brogues (which I thought were ever so dull). Ramsgate was the nearest town to Gram's farm. It had a cinema and a ballroom where they taught dance lessons. Mum said, since I turned fourteen, I could take lessons. The shops were ever so lovely, with layers of thick, creamy paint in bright yellows, greens, and reds; they all sat on a hill right over the harbour.

When we parked and began to walk along the lane, we found no one about. The walks and streets were empty. Then, for the first time, we heard the boom of guns out in the Channel. Coming down the slope of the block, I was a bit ahead of Mum and I saw the strangest thing. Down at the harbour, there were all kinds of ships parked, tied up beside each other. There was a loud, terrible commotion. All along the quay there were soldiers, some in bandages, many on stretchers, some limping into queues. They had torn dirty uniforms and tired faces. With the boom of the guns beyond, something thrilled through me. I said outloud, "I say! I'm really in a war!"

Mum caught up and looked at me crossly, "Elizabeth! I can't believe my ears!" Then she followed my gaze down to the quay and cried, "Merciful Heavens! It's our boys!" Grabbing my arm, Mum pulled me into the grocery store. She bought up what was left of the chocolate, biscuits, and cigarettes. We hurried along with our bundles to the quay.

It seemed the whole town was there. Women were giving out sandwiches, hot chocolate, and tea. They cheered, "Well done boys!" or "Well done BEF!" Some of the older men were delivering blankets, socks, and underwear. Oh my, who would have thought of underwear? Mum and I moved up the queue, passing out our small offering. Then we helped the other women. Oh those poor men! They were a sorry lot, grimed and whiskered, smelling of oil, with bits of sand stuck on their beat-up faces, and raggedy uniforms. But they actually smiled when we gave them the food. Frightfully lovely smiles.

"Where are they going?" Mum asked a lady passing out sandwiches.

"They're taking them to the trains. After, I don't know. Some say up north, some say Wales. The ones doing poorly, they go to hospital. No one knows where."

As Mum went on with this woman about the war, my eyes wandered to the ones in stretchers. The soldiers looked like broken dolls. Legs and arms bent and jutted in odd positions. Blood had soaked through their dressings and the blankets stuck to the blood. Their faces looked painted with grey-black grease and the rust colour of their blood; they were twisted up in a ghastly way, like the faces of discarded marionettes. I thought I would be ill. I wanted to run away.

It was then that I saw him. I stepped up the line of stretchers to have a look. He was lying beneath a blood-soaked red blanket. His face was black with dirt and oil. I knew it was oil because I could smell it. His eyes were closed, but as I bent over him, he looked up. I'd know him anywhere —the love of my life. I began to cry loudly.

"Mummy! Mummy, it's our Colley!" I alarmed everyone with my screams.

Mum came straight away. We both bent closer, not quite sure this was really our Colley.

He looked up at us. His light blue eyes were like a southern sea. (I always used to say that to him, even though I have never been to a southern sea.) We called out at once, "Colley, what are you doing here?" He stared.

"Colley lad, what are you doing here?" Mum asked, more gently, smoothing his blonde hair. It was stiff with grime and her fingers stuck to it. "Where's your mum and dad, love?"

Colley looked bewildered. He opened his mouth slightly, but not a sound came out. I could not stop crying. To hear my own voice, oh, it was like a high scream. My dearest friend was going to die. He looked like all the others down the row in stretchers. My tears fell on his face. He blinked up at me and moved his mouth.

"The lad can't hear you. He's deaf and dumb, miss, been hit pretty hard." A young military man dressed in khakis appeared beside us. "Know him, do you?"

"Yes, we're nearly family." Mum's voice was faint. She stroked Colley's hair and face.

"Could he be a Sea Scout? This lad?"

"No," Mum said. "Why?"

"Well, this one was in the *Malcolm*, if I'm not mistaken. Off one of them boats that went to help with the evacuation. Only one or two young civilians have been seen. They were Sea Scouts, you see."

"What do you mean? Boats went to help? Civilian boats?" Mummy asked.

"Small craft from all over England, they come to help rescue the BEF from the beaches. The Navy didn't have enough ships. And those they had, well, they couldn't get up close to the beaches. Too big, draw too much water. The waters are shallow, you see."

Mum said, "You mean fine yachts? Sailboats? They went too?"

"Everyone that's got seaworthiness. Ordered by Winston Churchill. I wonder…could you give us his name? Particulars? His parents? Address?" He said this, looking about; he was in a hurry. At that moment, a rough officer came up and ordered him off to another duty.

Mum called after him. But he did not look back. There were such noises and confusion, as rows of the soldiers that could walk started off up the quay. We were surrounded by soldiers gathering round the stretchers. They swooped down over Colley and lifted his stretcher. Mum and I ran after them, underfoot and squeezing between the soldiers. Mum pulled her shopping list and pencil from her bag. She wrote something down. When we reached Colley's stretcher, Mum called up to the bearers. "Where is he going?"

"Don't know," one answered.

"Please, can you take this? It has his name and address."

He tipped his head toward Colley, "Me hands is full. Can you just tuck it there? If you'll pardon, mum…" He pressed on with the rest.

Mum ran up along Colley's stretcher and stuffed the paper under his red blanket as he was marched away from us. A moment later, the note slipped away and flew under the trampling feet. We tried to get to Colley, but the crowds held us back.

Soldiers streamed past, making little eddies round us as if we were tiny rocks in a swift river.

* * * *

December 1940

Christmas was rather awful with Daddy gone. Mummy was sad. Gram still put up decorations, but she was not happy, like she used to be.

Mum searched for Colley every time she went on volunteer duty. She was driving for the government. She called on officials and visited hospitals. She found out that the Nevilles went missing in the Channel, but no proof, or anything like that. She discovered that lots of people went missing in action, and turned up home for tea, sometime later. We had hopes that the Nevilles would turn up for tea any day. Soon, we learned more.

One morning, our old neighbour, and my playmate, Mallory McCay, came for a visit. The McCay family had moved up to Scotland when the bombing started, and we had not heard much from them in some time. I did miss awfully our holidays with the Nevilles and the McCays. I remember how we all loved to go fishing in Gram's river. Oh, I would've given anything to be swimming with Colley and Mal in Gram's pond! And when Doctor Neville's boat was finished enough to sail, we went sailing. We three families had planned to sail on a round the world cruise. Oh, it was ever so lovely then.

Anyway, Mal surprised us when he came. He was home on leave. We hadn't seen him in over a year. Oh, he looked awfully grand in uniform, with all the brass. I hid by the staircase watching. Mum and Gram each took an arm and ushered him into the parlor (which we never used). He sat in my grandfather's wing-backed chair by the fireplace, across from Mum. I could hear Gram fussing in the kitchen.

"Liz-Beth? Come light the fire," Mum said. Mum's voice sounded happy for the first time in ever so long.

I'm sure I looked a fright in these woolen trousers and my grey woolen jumper. "Liz-Beth! Don't be rude," Mum called. I crossed the hall, smoothing down my hair. I had tied my hair with rag curlers the night before. I think it was quite fetching. I stretched the jumper down over my stomach (which I thought was too fat), and went into the parlor.

Mal got up and held out his arms. "Lizzy! Give us a hug!"

Well, I thought I would die of embarrassment right there. Mum laughed. Mal jumped at me, picked me up like a doll and twirled me around.

I cried, "Mal, put me down! You've ruined my hair!" He set me down and stood with his hands on his waist looking me over. I patted my hair back into shape. "And I hate you when you call me 'Lizzy'. My name's Elizabeth." I wondered…*did Mal fancy me?*

"Oh, so now are we a grown-up, top-drawer, top-brass, little princess?" He laughed. "Mal…" I crossed my arms over my chest. I could not think of anything clever to say. I thought I was quite grown-up. But my face felt red-hot; I knew it showed.

Gram set out tea, cakes, biscuits, cheese from our Jerseys, our ever-precious butter, and oh yes, ale from our brewer down the lane, which Mal enjoyed straightaway. It was indeed a feast; we did have plenty of these luxuries on the farm, but it soon became rare. Gram scooted her chair close and knitted.

Then Mal told us about Colley, how brave he was. How the guns were going off all around. How Colley didn't sleep the whole time. Days! Mal didn't actually see Doctor and Mrs. Neville get hit. He only saw Colley in the water. The smoke was so bad, he said. And when it cleared, there was just the boat, sailing itself away, like a ghost ship, Mal said. It gave me shivers.

Mal leaned back in the chair and lit a cigarette.

"And no one knows exactly what happened to the Nevilles?" Mum asked. "We've had no word of a memorial, or any official word on anything, really. And to find Colley, I've tried everything. There seems to be no hope. I'd been told that many of the hospitals had been bombed in the industrial regions and patients have been moved rather a lot."

Mal said, "With the war on and all, it's quite impossible finding one's kin. Our friends are all over the country. You know, of course, Mum and Dad are up in Scotland. The Nevilles, I don't think they had living relatives that we knew. They were lost in the Great War. I believe, however, there was a half-sister. Dr. Neville had a brief affair with a Canadian nurse. She was transferred home and came up pregnant. I guess the doctor supported the child all this time. She is close to Colley's age."

"Well! Colley may be with her? Where is she? What's her name?"

"If he made it," Mal said, watching the smoke curl. He was angry, I felt, or was he sad? I didn't really know.

"Of course he made it," Mum said.

"He was in a bad way when we fished him out of the water," Mal said.

"But we saw him!" I cried.

"I know Lizzy, your mummy told me." Mal looked into the fire and sucked his lower lip, the way he did when he was younger. "I gathered information. Colley being a civilian made it difficult, you see. And me being out to sea, too. I heard somewhere that the half-sister's in Canada. Her name is Cecily."

"Well then," Mum said, "we'll go straightaway and find our Colley." I was happy then. We would find our Colley.

Mal rubbed his red hair, thinking. "Canada is a big country."

"It's a million miles away," I started to cry. Everything was horrid. This war. The Nevilles. Colley, the man that I was sure I would marry. Gone. All gone.

Mum looked down at her empty teacup. "Well, perhaps we can find out more. We'll write letters, dears. We'll find him again, I know it." We all went quiet.

Mum said, "What about the boat? Perhaps the Nevilles were indeed aboard and may be safe somewhere. Well, they could arrive any minute for tea! Colley may have fallen overboard and…" Big tears filled her eyes, but they did not fall down.

"No hope, Mrs. Whitehead. The *Marie Celine* was spotted sailing herself. The witnesses were fairly shaken by the spectacle. She sailed on. Shells went off all around her. Water from the detonations geysered up tall pillars, and gunfire peppered the water. Swells from other ships and bombs created big rolling wakes. She sailed through, as if she were a phantom. As if nothing could touch her."

"Then, *Marie Celine* is out there somewhere. Colley would want to know. It would make him better. Make him come back to us. Our Colley," I said to the ceiling.

Mal shifted in his chair and pulled out another cigarette. "Lizzy love, no traces of *Marie Celine* have been found. The boat is classified as An Unfound Ship."

When Mal was leaving, he saw me, Mum and Gram looking queer. To cheer us up, he promised to come back on his next leave. He said he would have a car and take us for a ride. He said he would still look out for any information on our Colley and the *Marie Celine*, "An Unfound Ship." A great gloom settled over us.

SEVEN

Back of Beyond

January 1942. Colin Neville
St. Mary's Hospital, Exeter, England

*T*HE DOCTORS WROTE that my parents were missing in action. And I realized that I was utterly alone. No one was left. Between two world wars, my whole family had been annihilated.

Lying in hospital for all those months, I was haunted every night by nightmares, nightmares that would probably last for the rest of my life. One, most vivid, was a fighter plane bursting through the windows, into my ward, guns firing, right up to my bed. I could see the pilot's face. Then I would wake, frightened to death, watching the windows. I did not sleep again on those nights. When dawn came, I felt safe.

Another dream, not violent, but most distressing, was of a girl. I saw her at different stages of growth. Sometimes, she was little, three years old maybe? She ran through drying hops. It must have been harvest time, October? And I saw her, again as a little girl, standing naked in the sunlight, feeding apples to work horses. At first I thought she was in danger and the giant hooves would step on her. But the horses were kindly, and they reached with their long necks to take apples from her tiny hands. I dreamed of fruit orchards, a little boy and girl sitting in deep grass, wheat-coloured hops drying on racks, silver-white clouds, and fields of cattle and sheep, so brilliant…yet I could not remember where or who.

There was another dream where I was lying on a wharf over a lake. A pretty girl was in the lake calling me. But I wouldn't, or couldn't, move. Then this red-haired, freckled bully runs up behind me and forces me up facing the girl and she shrieks, then falls into peels of laughter, and I would wake, most times with an embarrassing and painful erection.

I spent my waking hours concentrating on piecing together the dream fragments; they were hints; they were clues somehow connected to my past.

I had no memory of Dunkirk. I recall a dream of *Marie Celine* sailing away from me.

Other than those glimpses back, I had only this new present. The doctors said that a little section of my brain had been temporarily barricaded off, like a road in repair, and the rest of the brain was doing detours around it. They said my symptoms were similar to those of battle fatigue, or shell shock, and that I should get well, soon.

I had been trapped in casts from my ankles to my shoulder blades for months. One bullet had lodged in my left knee, and I took bullets in my left thigh, my left shoulder, right buttocks, right ankle, and left hip. I couldn't speak and I couldn't hear. The doctors said that this phase of shock syndrome would also go away. The world was muffled and tranquil. Actually, I had no desire to speak, and I had no desire to hear. It was safe, this world, where other chaps came and went in bandages. I wasn't chummy with them — it was painful to try any sort of communication. In the end, they were always claimed — taken home by somebody or covered and carried down to the morgue. I was left to witness the new rounds of patients admitted to my ward.

When they removed the casts, I had to learn to walk again. It was about this time my half-sister Cecily popped up. Of course, at that time I had no idea who this young woman was, except that she was beautiful.

It was as if Christmas came into my grey and chilly ward. All the other chaps watched as she flowed up to my bed. Long scarves of bright reds, greens, aqua, and purples sailed off her shoulders. Cecily bent over me. Oh my, she was an orchard of fragrances—orange blossoms, bananas, passion fruits, and limes. She stared curiously into my face, furrowing her thin, tweezed brows. Then she clapped her hands and sang out, "Right, Colley, lad! It's wakey-wakey, shaky-shaky time! Do hurry, love-love, we will be late for the aeroplane." Of course, I couldn't hear a thing. It looked to me that she was singing a song of some sort. A sister off to the side motioned frantically to Cecily, who then paused dramatically, pulled a notepad from her jacket pocket, and wrote down the words. I nodded vigorously; all the hope in the world was suddenly born in this newfound young woman. Finally, someone had come for me. Not just anyone, a genie released from some wonderful land.

Cecily wore a long, grey, wool skirt of a homespun weave and a creamy blouse. Over that, a wool jacket hung loosely, and beneath these textures were the most marvelous leather boots. She had sorrel-red hair, all done-up in twists and loose rolls, secured with ornate combs. She was tall and slim, and I noticed that she was not just a pretty type— she was a handsome type. There was nothing scatty about Cecily. I dare say she exuded rich and exotic. I'd never seen anything like her, and I would have gone anywhere with her. To the end of the earth, I secretly vowed. Until I found that the end of earth (that is, earth as I knew it then) was just where she was about to take me: The Back of Beyond.

EIGHT

The Unfound Ship

1998 Colley's workshop
South Point Island, Nova Scotia.

*A*S I SAT carving a piece of wood into a ship's hull, I was thinking: *Marie Celine* was somewhere, waiting for me. She was my secret world, a vital key to what my life could have been, and a key to my past, a key to a person inside me that had never been revealed. My reliance on *Marie Celine's* existence walked with me on the pine needle floor of the ancient forest, held me steady as I climbed the slate blue rocks by the cove, worked with me in the lodge kitchen, sat with me in my studio, and kept me company when the kids had a go at me. It was another place into which I slipped, a place that no one could reach.

A dream of her haunted my life, a dream in which I save her. I sail her away to freedom. And in the act of saving her, she saves me. I regain that lost part of my life that hides deep in the caverns of my memory. At my age I am still waiting…expecting.

Cici always understood that part of me. She never asked about Dunkirk. My voice and hearing came back, but that period during the evacuation of Dunkirk was still a barricaded road in my mind, with all the detours in my brain still in place. Whistling tea kettles were banned from the kitchen, for Cici realized that von Richthofen toy whistles on the bombs had traumatized me. She was very wise, for I didn't know why the noise caused me to take cover at that time. Didn't know why the smell of gasoline and hot oil bothered me so. I did get off the crutches. However, I had a pronounced limp, favouring my left leg, to the point where many considered me a "gimp" (not in a bad way, mind you, it was simply their way of describing me). The pieces of metal lodged in my buttocks and thighs pained me at times, especially since I lived on the pine- and spruce-shaded, fog-shrouded South Point. To move to a dry climate, away from Cici? That was out of the question.

In fact, to leave the lodge for any reason was upsetting for me. In the absence of people my mind stilled, and someday I knew the past would flow quietly back through my memory. I even avoided going to the village for supplies. I rarely left this island. So, to many of our neighbours, I was considered not only a "gimp", but a "shut-in" as well. No worries. I did what was needed about our place, herding goats and sheep over bridges and causeways to our neighbour islands to graze, shearing sheep, milking goats, fixing pumps, cooking, and even spinning wool with the local ladies. Our little lodge was busy enough in the summer with kayakers and nature enthusiasts to keep us in good shape. The wool and weaving business supported us during the winter.

I smiled quite a bit, and mused on what wonder has passed in my life: my late wife, Alice, my daughter, Anne, and my magical Cici who, all alone, made our lodge the destination for artists on retreat, canoe folk, and kayakers.

And as I sat whittling, occasionally I looked out the bench windows to the fractured morning sunlight on the mossy trail leading over from the lodge; it dappled the bridge and speckled the porch. I was very strongly into my expectant mood. I knew something was going to happen. Perhaps this day I would see something, or hear something, that might connect me with the missing piece of my life. I felt it in my sore bones. I could smell it in the rain-sodden leaf mulch, in the crusty, musty bark of black spruce, the spicy new needles of white pines, and in the smouldering embers in the fireplace. I could hear it in the rush of the swollen, spring tides, crashing over rocks beside the front porch.

I rested the model on the workbench and gazed out the mismatch of barn-paned windows that made up most of the south wall. I had heard the first flock of Canada geese fly over the island the other day. Home for spring. The geese always gave me a new hope. The spring sun had just reached her zenith; gold ribbons weaved through pine branches and diffused over the room. It set a golden dust on worn, wide, oak floor-planks, and on settees built like bunks on a sailing ship. Gold sprinkled over the maple furniture and sprayed the east side of the studio that I had built as a ship's bridge, with binnacle, wheel, and windows facing the Atlantic horizon. The glow spilled to the shelves cluttered with stacks of tattered books: Compton Mackenzie, Mark Twain, Dickens, Robert Louis Stevenson, Arthur Ransom, books on boat building, model boat building, and making ships in bottles. Set between books were wood clamps, awls, nail sets, glue pots, miniature drills, band saws, back saws, coping saws, armadas of ship models, and most notably, the butterscotch sun beamed on my half-model of *Marie Celine*. The first spring sun did not bring much warmth, but it brought new light.

I caught my reflection in the bench windows. Like a fleeting shadow with a light brushstroke here and there, a figure sat—tall, slim and bent over the workbench. A longish Saxon face, bony, with a Roman nose and thick, tangled white hair and brows. Against the light on the panes, the eyes were dark blanks. But I've been told, those pale blue eyes had the look of a seeker. I wondered: who was I really? So many questions Ci cannot answer. Was I always going to be an empty being? A young soul?

I left my stool and shuffled across the room, then waited for Black Dog and Yellow Dog to move away from the fireplace. I sat in the rocking chair, leaned forward and lazily pulled some logs from the woodpile to toss on the embers. The dogs stretched, scratched and resumed their positions by the hearth. Looking around, I marveled at the newness of everything, as if I had sensed it for the first time. I wanted to remember this room, this time, the first spring sun.

"Colley! Colley-love-love! Coll—eeey!"

Really. I was just getting comfortable. Was it time for me to do the prep-cooking already? Maybe something had gone wrong down at the lodge. The well pump had been screeching for a bearing. Stiffly, getting up from the chair, I moved across the room and opened the top of the Dutch door. The dogs crowded around my legs, yipping that excited bark that welcomes a loved one. There was dear Cici, marching across the bridge in her Eskimo boots, long cotton dress and handmade wool shawl draped from shoulders to ankles, lifting in the breeze like a magician's cloak. Cici's hair was dyed-red, with pink highlights in the sun. She still wore it up. This day she had it pinned in place with fancy chopsticks that had sequined aqua tassels.

Behind her was a man. He wasn't a local artist-type. Not one of our island men either. Not a government man (though we've had a few of those misguided ninny-heads skulking around our island in the past). No, this chap looked like what Cici and I call "The City." He had that short hairstyle that my Annie and her mates describe as "edgy," and he had wire-rimmed round spectacles hanging off a rather hooked nose. He wore new dungarees, doe-coloured suede hiking boots (which had never seen mud, rocks, or slippery moss), a black T-shirt, a black leather loose-fitting blazer, and he carried a new, black leather briefcase.

Cici was slightly breathless when she reached the top of the porch. "Colley-love! There's a chap…" She waved her hand vaguely towards the bridge, where the visitor paused.

"Yes, Cici love, I can see there's a chap." Reluctantly, I motioned him on.

Cici appeared flustered. Her thin red brows popped up, painted eyes widened. "Colley-love-love, he insisted on following me over. Wouldn't wait in the lodge, you see." She had done her eyes in turquoise glitter that day, and her cheeks were powdered plum, her lips rouged a darker plum, all this against alabaster skin that had seen every beauty treatment and anti-aging potion that came over the South Shore mail route.

I opened the bottom half of the door just as the visitor stepped up on the porch. The dogs rushed out, announcing company. Automatically, Cici hooked their collars and held them back. "Colley-love, this is Mr., oh dear, it has indeed eluded me."

"Graydon, Gidney Graydon. CBC Television, Halifax." He skirted the nuzzling, drooling dogs, holding his briefcase high, as if wading through waist-deep water. Reaching over the dogs' noses, he thrust his right hand forward, "Mr. Colin Neville?" I nodded. He shook my hand vigorously. "Mr. Neville, I've been a long time finding you. I have news that I think will be of interest."

Up close, he looked to be in his fifties. Brushing sawdust off my denim work shirt and jeans, I motioned him to have a seat, and sent the dogs down the hill.

I added more logs to the fire. Flustered, Cici went to forage refreshments in my galley-kitchen. Watching the flames, I quickly tried to ascertain the reason for a visit with me, in this remote part of the world, from a rather natty-looking city-type. Scanning my studio, Graydon sank into the lumpy stuffing of the armchair, and then leaned forward expectantly. "Mr. Neville, have you seen our special series on the Battle of Britain? The preview of the first episode ran last month. Big project. Been going on for quite a while."

"As you see, Mr. Graydon, we don't have a television."

He looked round. "You must have one down at the lodge? In the rental cabins?"

"People who want that sort of thing stay at the mainland resorts."

Cici set a tray on the coffee table, and passed out bread, goat cheese, and glasses of some of our homemade blueberry wine. "We may have been isolated," she sniffed, "but now, world travelers, artists, writers come here to visit." She took another breath. "Since we have the ferry…"

Noticing a flicker of anxiety cross Graydon's face, I put in, "I am sorry, we've gone on. You came here on a mission."

"Oh, no, really. It's all very interesting. A rare perspective you've had of the world, I'm sure." Frowning, Graydon looked at the thick slice of coarse, country bread and rough white cheese sandwiched between his fingers. "That explains why it was so hard finding you guys." Pre-occupied, he set the bread back on the plate. "A colleague of mine spent a week here, at one of your Natural Arts seminars. He picked up on some conversation about your past, Mr. Neville. After quite lengthy research, I think you're my man. Or should I say boy?"

I shrunk in my chair, "Pardon?"

He brightened. "Yes!" Graydon pushed his glasses up to the bridge of his nose, brought up his briefcase and riffled through the contents. He retrieved some papers and arranged them on his lap, tapping the stack in place. "I know who you are and where you've been. People are looking for you." He paused, "I know about *Marie Celine*." His attention was riveted suddenly on the half-model of *Marie*.

It was too much. My eyes fell to the bits of bark and ashes around the hearth. Graydon waited, then asked, "Mr. Neville? Are you okay?"

Cici got up, stood behind me, and placed her arms about my neck. "Colley-love?" She turned to Graydon. "Mr. Graydon, this may not be good for my Colley. There are things that should not be remembered. I've worked hard all these years to keep him safe from the past. Too much, you see?" I felt her arms tighten on my shoulders.

I again heard that buzzing and ringing in my ears. I couldn't speak. My hands shook. Then, just as suddenly as they came, the noises in my ears faded and I heard my voice again, weakly, "I am quite right, actually. Mr. Graydon, can you tell me exactly what you mean?"

Graydon, noting my tremors, asked, "Are you sure?"

"Quite."

Beaming with discovery, he spoke in staccato. "I've been researching the archives in England for our piece on the Battle of Britain. My assignment was the miraculous evacuation of the British Expeditionary Force from the beaches of Dunkirk. A fleet of small personal craft, called the Little Ships, or as Churchill called them, 'The Mosquito Armada,' saved those soldiers. I interviewed a lot of guys from the, um," he referred to his notes, "Veteran's Association of Dunkirk. There is this story about a boy, a teen, who did heroic deeds. He is the one I am looking for. He was in one of the Little Ships, a sailing yacht, with his family. The yacht was identified as the *Marie Celine*.

"'Heroic deeds?'" I echoed dully.

"These veterans saw this kid on the beach, guns going off all around him, helping soldiers into boats and rowing them to the sailing vessel. Bombs everywhere. And the mystery: the boy disappeared, the family disappeared, and soldiers reported that they saw the boat sailing herself through the Channel, 'like an avenging angel' they said, 'Clean and white as could be, against a world of war. Nothing touched her.'"

"They saw her sailing herself?" I said. I thought perhaps I'd been a bit crazy all these years, with the memory of seeing that last image of *Marie Celine* sailing herself away.

Graydon hurried on. "Yeah, it was the strangest thing. Many of the soldiers saw her at different times, at different parts of the Channel. One group in a barge said they saw her sitting like a statue on a sandy shoal at Bray-Dunes. A few of the guys I interviewed said they saw her heading out to sea. Remarkable! Of course, some said it was the tide that carried her. Others said, surely she didn't make it. She'd have to have been shot up. But, after that, there were more sightings! Off the coast of France…and further sightings…" Graydon became suddenly agitated. "Mr. Neville, there has been an association since the sixties, called the Association of Dunkirk Little Ships. They have a subgroup tracking these Little Ships such as *Marie Celine*. It is called The Unfound Ships. Haven't you heard anything about this? *Marie Celine* is an Unfound Ship. She could be out there somewhere!"

Cici squeezed me. "Let's not, love."

I took her hand and guided her to the cushion beside me. "We'll be alright, Ci." And then to Graydon, "As you now know, I have been rather isolated. Do please, press on."

At this instant the Dutch door rattled open. "What's everybody doing up here?" Anne left the door ajar and slouched into the room. The dogs tumbled in behind her. The wet cuffs of her baggy pants dragged across the floor, gathering dust and balls of dog hair. She said,

"Selig's in the kitchen going crazy. There're people in the dining room. Come in from off the ferry." She then saw Graydon standing by his chair, a gentleman waiting for an introduction.

I said, "Mr. Graydon, this is Anne Neville, my daughter, the student who is supposed to be in school today."

"Hello Anne," Graydon held out his hand.

Anne murmured, "Oh, hi." She shook his hand.

Distracted, Graydon pushed his glasses back onto the bridge of his nose. "Mr. Graydon is from a TV station," I said.

"Which one?" She straightened with interest, tossing the hank of blond hair off her face.

"CBC."

"Oh, cool. What are you doing here? Another famous guest, like, hiding out at the old lodge?"

"Your father. He is the famous one."

"My dad?" She paused and looked around, "Oh, yeah, you mean for his carvings and stuff?"

A shadow crossed Cici's face, as she looked from Anne to me.

Graydon explained. "Not quite. It's something far greater. I have come to request a televised interview with your father to be aired on our special on the Battle of Britain."

"Oh-my," I said.

Cici said, "That will never do."

Bewildered, Anne burst out, "But why? He can't remember anything." Anne let out a sigh that seemed to deflate, then bend, her willowy form as if beneath an awful weight. Her shoulders slumped, "Really."

Cici huffed, "Right, lass, now go to the kitchen and wait for us." Anne shuffled out, the dogs clamouring after her.

Graydon stood self-consciously, with a half-smile, half-grimace. "Please sit down, Mr. Graydon," I said.

Cici threw up her hands. Her shawl winged the air. She folded into her chair and sat primly, chin resting in palm.

Graydon returned to his seat and thumbed through sheaves of paperwork. "I have filmed interviews with people who remember you, Mr. Neville. They knew you. They remember everything: your valour, your endurance, your optimism. They were saved by you and the mystery boat, *Marie Celine*."

I sat back in my chair, shaking my head, "But I can't remember, really. I could ruin your affair."

"The deal is, Mr. Neville, you are the most important key. You are important to these men you helped save. If anything, it would help them just to see you, to know that you are alive. Mr. Neville, there are not many of these soldiers left, you know. You are a part of history. You may have clues to the whereabouts of the *Marie Celine*. We will not put you under any stress, whatsoever. If you become uncomfortable, I will stop the session."

I told Graydon that I needed time. He said I did not have much. We agreed to talk within the week.

We accompanied him over the bridge to the lodge. I gazed up. The sky was Easter egg blue. My favorite sky. And to top it off, white, almost phosphorescent, clouds streaked in three straight lines across the blue. "Have a look...look at those beautiful clouds!"

Graydon glanced up, squinting against the glare. Cici studied Graydon a second, waiting. He looked down at no one in particular, and let out a short disbelieving laugh, "Contrails. I'll be damned. I never thought of the poetry of contrails. I'll think of that every time I see them now: "What beautiful clouds!" He watched the silver streaks, shaking his head and musing happily, "What beautiful clouds!"

I grinned and took another gander at the heavens. Cici smiled indulgently at Graydon. We moved on to the back door of the kitchen. With one look at the chaos in the kitchen, Graydon declined lunch and was on his way back to The City.

NINE

The Decision

THE KITCHEN WAS a mess. Black Dog and Yellow Dog sprawled by the prep island. Selig, our handy man, swearing in Polish, stepped over them, while balancing a load of food from the walk-in. Sausages skipped on the floor. He tucked a roast beef under his arm like a midget football player and trudged on. Tomatoes jumped from the load and rolled across the kitchen.

Anne slipped into an apron and ducked out into the dining room. She flew back into the kitchen. "There's a bunch of people! No one has any food, yet."

The first good day of spring must have inspired tourists to venture out.

Tying her apron, Cici read the orders clipped above the stove. "Don't get your knickers in a twist, lass. Give them bread and butter. Fill water glasses."

Grumbling, Anne set up plates of bread. The visit from Graydon had upset our routine; it also upset me. I needed time to think about Graydon's message. Since he left, odd pictures had floated through my mind. I was not sure if they were memories finding their way back to the main roads of my brain, or dreams I'd had, or simply disjointed illusions. I was suspended between fear of the unknown and joy of discovery.

I manned my station at the butcher's block and set the chef's knife to dicing vegetables.

The rhythm of the blade tapping wood sent the noise and confusion away from me. From my corner of the universe, I watched Anne trudging back and forth with plates of cold beef and grilled tomatoes. She was still young for her age, underdeveloped. All the young girls on the island seemed to fill out at about the same time; Anne didn't. As she moved across the kitchen, I saw that she had become taller. But her antelope quarters, long thin arms and legs, and high waist were quite visible poking through those army surplus togs, like bones in a gunnysack. Baggy tops did not conceal her flat chest either. As disinterested as she appeared to be toward life, there was something wonderful and untapped in her. That fawn-coloured skin, fine-boned little face with the high forehead, and white-blonde hair, glowed with youth and newness. No matter how she tried to reject it, Anne had a purity about her that shone. I wondered if she would ever find her niche in life.

Anne was a baby when my young wife died, so she didn't know her mum. Cici and I were her parents. No one on the island thought us too old to be parents at that time.

When Anne left the schoolhouse on the island, we sent her to the Sacred Heart boarding school in Halifax.

From there, we sent her over to the most expensive Catholic girls' college in Nova Scotia. She changed her majors from art to archeology, from biology to astronomy, from political science to the lofty major of French Literature, out of which she flunked. The first years at the college were tumultuous, to put it mildly. She was put on probation every semester.

And here she was, home.

After the lunch guests cleared out, Anne, Selig, Cici and I sat down for a drink. Abruptly, Cici asked, "So, what did you do this time? Why didn't we hear from Sister Ambrose?"

"The phone wasn't working," Anne said.

Selig wrinkled his banana nose, "She's right," and took a long pull on his beer.

Cici looked to me, questioning. "True," I said. "It was dead for a time. Some new cable thing going on. Remember?" Cici nodded, not convinced.

Anne said, "You need to buy a mobile phone."

"Customers say they can't get a signal here," I said. "Anne, at the end of the day, I don't think you tried very hard."

Anne rolled her eyes. Cici persisted. "So, what did you do this time?"

"I dropped out!"

"Oh dear," Cici sighed pressing her fingers on her temples. "Now you've really muddled things up."

Anne crossed her arms. "You all taught me to be a free thinker," she accused. "Well, I think I hate school. That's how I really feel."

I cringed.

"I have to go call Sister Ambrose," Cici said faintly.

"It won't do any good. I don't want to go back there. It's like some medieval prison. In fact, I don't want to go anywhere. I'm staying right here."

"Anne, you don't have to go anywhere. We can cast about and find a school that fits you," I said.

"I don't want to go to school anymore. I don't fit anywhere. I fit right here," she added with a desultory effort.

Cici and I exchanged apprehensive glances.

That night, after the dinner shift, Selig poured a glass of port for Ci, fluffed up her settee pillows, then went home to his brood. The few guests we had that night retired to their cabins.

Cici, Anne and I sat at the kitchen table for our traditional late supper. For a skinny girl, she was eating mounds of vegetables. "I'm a vegetarian now." She gulped down a diet cola.

"No wonder you're so thin," I said, "and those baggy jeans don't help your figure."

"Hum," Anne said, crunching thoughtfully on raw carrots, "so what's happening with that CBC guy?"

I poured another dram of Scotch. "I have made a decision," I said. "In the morning I'm calling Graydon. I'm going to do the interview."

There was a gasp.

Cici said, "Why on earth would you do that, Colley?"

"Don't know, actually. I feel it is important. I feel I must do it."

"Dad, I'm sure," Anne sighed deeply.

"I could use some support on this matter. I could use some help… shoring up, as it were. Anyone?"

"Humph." Anne left the room.

Cici collected the dishes shaking her head. The next morning, I called Graydon.

TEN

A New Life

*T*HE LODGE BECAME an encampment for Graydon and his film crew. Late one Tuesday afternoon, they arrived in vans filled with cable, wires, booms, and lighting. They set up in my cabin. Graydon thought it an ideal background, the nautical ambiance of the cabin along with the ship models and other carvings. It was quite an invasion. However, Cici loved it—the hustle, the noise, and the company. Anne prepared several cabins for our new guests and worked the restaurant and kitchen with Cici.

I had been extremely apprehensive about this whole event. Now I felt a slow panic. What if I couldn't remember anything? What if I lost my voice and my hearing again? What if Anne and Cici—along with the rest of the world—saw me waver, falter, and fall to pieces? Graydon promised that if I had problems, he would cancel. My courage was, nevertheless, on the wane.

Until that evening, after dinner, when something queer happened.

Word got out on the mainland that we had a film crew from CBC staying at the lodge. So on that crisp midweek evening, many of the locals stopped in. An impromptu party started up in the bar. Folk musicians jammed. Fiddles, guitars, mandolins, Celtic drums. Celtic, country, and Acadian players competed with each other. Scottish, English, and French tunes rang out. Cici's hips were swinging, swishing her long gypsy skirt this way and that. Selig's white-fringed head nodded time to the music as he bussed tables and served drinks. Amused, Anne crossed her arms and leaned in the kitchen doorway.

A man with a white-haired ponytail gave Cici a turn around the dance floor. More couples joined in. One of the ancient ones from up the cape said, "Play a tune from Jolly Old England! Sing us 'Widecombe Fair.'" A Scotsman started up, singing a folk song about a grey mare and an English country fair. Cici and her dance partner joined in singing.

This folk song was a familiar tune to me, though I swear I'd never heard it. It hummed in my ears and ricocheted off the annals of my brain. For an instant, the room darkened and before me was the flotilla of Little Ships emerging from the fog. I saw Dad at the helm of *Marie Celine*.

The fog lifted and I was back in the bar. I noticed Cici pause and dart her head here and there, like a small bird, searching. Abruptly, she left her partner and found me leaning on the bar at the rear of the room. The lights caught tears brightening her eyes. She clutched my arm and said, "Colley love-love, are you right? Love, you look a bit crook."

My voice sounded hollow. "I'm all right," I said, trying to smile. She gave me a couple of pats, skittered up to the musicians and whispered. The players regrouped and began a sea chanty. Cici cast a few worried glances my way. I nodded and waved. Subdued, she went about serving customers.

I fixed my eyes on the space in the room where I had seen the vision. Matted over the dance floor was a beach. Soldiers were queued at the water's edge. I watched myself dive and cover my head as a mortar went off. Wet sand pelted me and, abruptly, everything went still. When I looked up, the group of soldiers was a mass of jelly. I shut my eyes. My cane clattered to the floor.

"Do you need help?" Graydon was suddenly there, supporting my arm.

"No worries." Slowly I bent, picked up the cane, straightened, and knocked down my Scotch. I said, "I'm ready, Graydon. We'd better go now. I'll have coffee sent up. It is going to be a long night. A lifetime in a night."

Graydon and I worked alone through the night and to the next evening. I recalled everything from leaving Ramsgate to seeing my parents die, to being picked up in the fiery water, to *Marie* sailing away. There were blank spots between the time I was in the lifeboat and when I awoke in hospital. In the early morning, the crew joined us and we worked throughout the day without a break, and without interruption.

Late that evening the crew, somber now, packed the vans. Graydon came down from the lodge. He clasped my shoulders and held me there, looking closely into my eyes, "Are you sure you'll be okay? You look shook up, man. Perhaps a doctor?"

I patted his arms, "Graydon, I will be quite right, you'll see. Good as gold. Right as rain."

Reluctantly he joined the group, and presently the vans and SUVs drove on the last ferry for the mainland. I watched them fade into the purple-black South Shore night. I watched the headlights beam out over the land as they drove off the ferry. Sounds of high surf hissed and snapped off the rock reefs.

I stood a long time and listened to the ocean. The water's surge was one of the first things I heard when I got my hearing back so long ago. It had frightened me then, that roar, building as it travelled up the gut by my cabin. I thought it would swallow me.

The moment I got my hearing back was the night I arrived here, at the lodge. Cici had put on a kettle for tea. I happened to be in the kitchen with her, by the stove. Steam from the kettle plumed. The Stuka's whistle came bearing down on me, as it crashed through the far wall, heading for me. Leaping from the chair, I dove under the table. In my ears, noises came from within me that did not sound human. Suddenly it all stopped and Cici was under the table holding me. I heard for the first time my sister's soprano voice.

"Colley! You can hear!"

And now, after all those years of not remembering, I remembered! Scenes were projected out of the darkness before me, like a carousel of brilliantly coloured slides. Squeezing my eyes shut, I shook off the shock and started up for the lodge. Halfway to the top, I noticed that I had been walking without the aid of my cane. I stood at the heavy pine doors pondering how I got up the hill without pain. Scents of damp grasses, pine needles and bread baking hung in the night air.

A life. Powerful life. I was a part of a family. I could look back and see us together laughing. I had a family I could talk about, cry about. I could find pieces of myself in Mum. I saw my tall, lanky figure in Dad. My love for boats. Mum, she loved fishing and I was getting pretty good at fly fishing. I could look at Anne and see her bony face... so like Dad's. And Ci's mouth tightened straight across in a thin line when she was determined, just like Dad. And I could tell Cici (who never met Dad) things about him that she never knew. It gave me great joy to supply the missing bits of our lives. I remembered, when I was small and beginning to walk, they caught me up on the decks heading for the rail. That's when they put netting across my bunk; it was my playpen. A mysterious small scar on my arm always puzzled me. I knew now, I got that catching my arm on a cotter pin in a turnbuckle. My world was *Marie Celine*. Staggered by this new life, I needed time to sort it out. And then I would have a plan. I would find *Marie Celine*. There was very little time left.

ELEVEN

CBC/BBC Special Aired

I HAD A DEADLINE for the Coast Gallery Folk Art Show. That gave me an excuse to hide in my cabin. I worked on the carvings and mused over my discoveries. Luckily the weather had turned bad and business was slow. Strangely enough, no one asked me about my experience with the interview. There were the odd polite mumbles. I was grateful.

One afternoon I heard the jeep motoring up the road; Anne was driving. I arrived at the window just in time to catch the jeep's rear end before it was out of sight; it was filled with a big box. I headed down to the lodge.

"Yes love-love, a television and VCR, and an extra phone line for the internet. Oh, and a black box. Everybody has a black box!" Cici, in her hot pink workout sweats, said this breezily, as she took her morning cuppa from the kitchen counter.

"But, but…to change our tradition…"

"No buts my love. We are now wired—that is the vernacular, I surmise—to the world."

She held her cup up to me, toasting. "Change is good! It keeps one young!"

All I could do was stare at her in amazement. The lodge was a sanctuary. We were keepers of the old ways. Conservationists, kayakers, bird watchers, all came here for the wilderness ambiance. Cici was the last of the Bohemians, owner of the last authentic retreat from the world, soon to be wound with wires. "Wired?" I cried. "Why, Earth is so wired, that from space it must look like a giant ball of string!" With that, Cici hurried from the kitchen on a sudden errand.

My stomach knotted. What had Graydon kept of the interview? We had talked on the telephone quite a bit since that night. He was a genuinely likable chap, very earnest and interested. He had asked me several more questions on the phone, some of which I could not answer. He did hit on one thing: he asked me if I remembered a soldier who had been in the boat with me who was known as "Crow." I explained that with the noise and the urgency of the situation, no one exchanged names. Then Graydon said this man was called Crow on account of his enormous nose and birdlike appearance. I clued in. Yes, I said, he was the one who told me about the sounds of the bombs. Graydon, in a state of excitement, rang off. He was on his way back to England.

I did not hear from Graydon again until he called to inform me of the date and time the first segment of the documentary would air. He said he could send down videotapes of the first two episodes, if we could find the equipment to play them on. I said, actually we did have it now. Sounding a bit surprised, he urged me to see them.

The film arrived by courier. We gathered in Anne's cabin. Cici was in a festive mood. A bit forced, I felt. Nevertheless, she flounced here and there, setting up plates of cheeses and pate, accompanied by good wines, not the usual *vin de pays*.

The programme began with background story of World War Two. The stills shown were absorbing—those long, panoramic shots picturing thousands of troops on the beaches. The enormity of the event came back to me like a slam. I could smell gunpowder, burning oil, blood. I could hear it, taste it. For a moment, I did not think I could watch any more.

Then the rescue story began: the evacuation of the British Expeditionary Forces from Dunkirk by the Little Ships.

The film cut to a close-up of my face.

"We were tied up at the boatyard," I said on screen. "We were going to get *Marie's* rigging redone for our cruise round the world. This cruise had been planned since Dad came home from the Great War, a young man.

"I was home from school on the weekend, I remember clearly. We were having tea down below. The owner of the boatyard came aboard. He was very calm. He said, 'Dr. Neville, there's trouble across the Channel. The *Marie Celine* is needed. Would you agree to take her?' We did not know what we were in for over there, but my dad agreed, of course.

"Orders were to empty all the boats. But we had no time to empty ours. A good thing too, for we had jerry cans for petrol and water, medical supplies that had been stored for our world trip…

"My parents sent me back to school. But I ran away and hid on the boat." My image dissolved.

The film continued. Evacuated veterans were being interviewed by a BBC announcer.

The withered visage of the man called "Crow" came into focus. His face was caved and puckered from lack of teeth. His nose was unmistakable, beaky and hooked at the end like a can opener. He was the same man who had been in the boat with me. With a Cockney accent, he told of the sleepless marches to the sea, to be rescued. "We reached the outskirts of Dunkirk. We were done in and ready to give up right then and there.

"Down at the beaches, hungry, parched from lack of fresh water, we were nearly dying from hours of bombing. Waiting like sitting ducks, we were, on the beach, for a boat to get us out. It was an awful sight. Fear, confusion.

"Then we got a boat. I thought to myself that we were surely dead now, when I saw this young lad, tall and skinny, a boy, mind you, manning our escape boat. He was wild-eyed and hardly stout enough to manage the high-railed lifeboat he had. What the hell, I thought, we're done for. Then the officers on the beach ordered us to board that boat. The boy, by God, knew his boats, and boarded our men without tipping the thing. And row, this laddy did. The blokes in the boat were landsmen. This lad got them up and rowing with him. The bombs got bad around us, and it's the first time I saw him break his stroke. His yellow hair stood up, halo-like, his eyes wide, he ducked every time he heard the bombs whistle. I told him, I said..."

And Crow described the escape from the beaches to our *Marie Celine*.

"When we reached the boat, the lad had to boost some of the weak ones up over the rail while those on deck helped them aboard. On the decks, I was felled from exhaustion. Didn't think, even then, I'd make it through this. This gent appeared kneeling in front of me. He had white hair and a fancy yacht suit. Top brass, you know. He set down a bucket of water, gave me a ladle of it and a piece of bread. Oh la, I never tasted anything so good. 'Buck-up!' he said, 'you're going home. You'll be on the five-o-clock train for London. Got to look your best, chappy.' They were the bravest lot, those people. I'd give anything to thank them. I thought of them all these years, and the spirit of that boat, how it helped us get home. And we were on that train. It didn't go to London, though. It took us to a camp where we made ready to fight again. But like the gent said, that sailboat did get us home. Home to England!"

That white-haired gent was my dad, of course, and I saw him as if he were in the room with me.

"That was you, that kid, aye Dad?" Anne asked. I told her it was.

Next, a bent man with one leg, swung forward on crutches, anxious to tell his story. He told of being left on the beach and of the one young lad who stopped to save him. He told of being carried off the beach and floated out to our boat. Oh my, it was that poor devil I couldn't leave behind.

After that, a close-up of a rather dapper-looking old chap in tweeds, with white thick hair and a silver, neatly trimmed beard was up on the screen. Behind him I saw a cozy Victorian-era library, a crackling fire, and on amber-toned walls was a collection of classical paintings. I peered at this man, "My God, that's Rutherford!"

Anne turned to me, "You know him, Dad?"

"By God, I do!" I sat forward, wishing I could jump into the screen. *Oh my, Rutherford. We have so much catching up to do.*

Rutherford was going on, in a clipped, educated accent, about the mess on the beach, and finally, he talked of the Little Ships. "Brave lads. They were average chaps, you see, all shapes and sizes. All completely unaware of the catastrophe going on here in France. They were as shocked to see us in our predicament as we were to see them in that ragtag flotilla." Then the interviewer asked if anything stood out for him during this ordeal. And Rutherford answered, "There was this young lad on the beach whom I'll never forget. "

And so he told the story of his experience with *Marie Celine*, of me and my parents. The camera fanned to another close-up of my face.

Did I have that stiff-upper-lip bit going, I wondered. I had never realized how *English* I sounded and how *English* my rather rigid, reserved countenance came over. Cici always commented on the purity of my accent, as if I had never left England…that slow, pensive, deliberate rhythm of speech that maintained, above all, a matter-of-fact undertone.

The camera pulled back to a wider angle. I was in my denim work-shirt, sitting on the bench stool with the barn-paned windows and shelves of models in the background. I looked slim and too tall; I seemed to hover over the workbench. Graydon, off camera, began the interview.

The lights were low. My face was spotlighted softly, with faint back-lighting on the studio. I told my story with a semblance of restraint, even distance. A few times my voice became ragged. I saw myself on screen, with an odd half smile, and tears shining in my eyes as I spoke. I told the story of Mallory McCay, Rutherford, the chap in the lifeboat called "Crow," and the poor devil at the water's edge with a shot-off leg. And all this with clarity and vivid recollection.

Graydon said to me, "These men all spoke of your bravery."

I replied, "I was so scared. Frightened to death, you see. There was nothing to do but do my job. I was scared into bravery, I suppose." And I gave a half smile.

When I came to the part when my parents were shot, my voice snagged. Now water spilled from my eyes. Suffused in grief, I carried on. At times I could not discern if it were a spasm of a rigid smile on my face, or a ghastly grimace. Often I turned my attention to the ceiling beams, the windows, the bookshelves, as I recounted what had happened. I said, "My hope was in *Marie Celine*. If I could reach her, I could reach my parents. If I could reach her, we would be together again. As Mal and Rutherford held me down in the lifeboat, *Marie* and hope sailed away from me forever. Then of course, I passed out from my injuries."

The camera pulled back to a long shot of me as I turned on the stool, rested my chin in my palm, and gazed at the model of *Marie Celine*.

There was an interlude of music. The tape had to be changed. But no one moved. After a bit, Anne changed the tape.

Cici was weeping and sputtering, "I lived all these years with impersonal phrases: 'Missing in Action,' or 'Gone Missing.' Oh, Colley, 'Missing' means they might have turned up, you see? Others did."

Discomfited, in this new position, I paused. For a black moment, I felt I had unleashed a monster on my family: my past.

The next segment contained alarming information about *Marie Celine*. The scene opened with a full shot of my model of *Marie Celine*. Then it cut to a withered, bent veteran wearing an ill-fitted suit dotted with medals and ribbons. He said, "Oh, she was out there. We saw her sailing out the Channel. It was dark, and the dive-bombers tried to dump their last bombs on her. They missed. But it sent the boat some pretty good waves from the blasts. After, we saw her shadow move on. Couldn't see a soul aboard."

The next frame gave me the shivers. Another face came into view that had the weathered, deeply wrinkled look of one who had been at sea all his life. "We was fishing and got blown off course near the Bay of Biscay, an' we saw a sailboat. A fancy yacht-like. She was pretty beat-up, but sailing fine. We had the glasses on her when a German boat came into our sights. Lucky for us, that patrol boat headed right for the yacht. We got the hell out of there."

"Oh, she's done for. That's it," Cici cried out.

"Maybe it was a ghost boat!" Anne was excited.

Another clue: a retired Special Operations Executive agent was introduced by the announcer. His well-preserved head with buzz-cut filled the screen. He was saying, "This soldier's aunt wouldn't let it go. She swore that he was alive. She brought us a handwritten message she received from him carried by one of our contacts in France. It said that her nephew, Rod Slater, had been saved by a sailboat and that he was injured, hidden in the South of France. A sailboat? Information, then, was difficult; the Vichy had come into power and the people of the south were divided by politics and regimes. No one could be trusted. There were intrigues and dissent, even among family members. That letter from Slater could have been code for all we knew. But we experimented with that theory. Nothing came of it. Our official information was that he, Slater, along with his unit, had been killed at Furnes, with the last of the rearguard. At any rate, we had no time for this sort of thing—even if he actually was saved by a sailboat and still alive."

A wobble went through my gut. Here were clues as to the whereabouts or the fate of my *Marie Celine*. I felt hope. I saw possibility.

Spellbound, we watched the tapes until sunrise.

Early morning light didn't hit Anne's cabin. Instead it made its pink presence on my cabin windows across the bridge. Those warped barn-panes reflected back a stained-glass window pattern of greens, yellow-pinks, and metallic oranges into Anne's living room.

I was roaming in my own memories; Anne's voice brought me back. "Dad?" Anne hesitated.

"Yes, love."

"I…I didn't have a clue."

"I didn't either, my Annie."

Cici was frozen in her chair, her tear-swollen eyes still on the blank TV screen.

Anne turned suddenly. "Dad, what if…she could be out there, somewhere." She went to the desk and turned on her computer.

"I thought you were tired. Don't you want some sleep? I'll feed the animals."

Without turning from the screen, she said, "Thanks. I'm going to… I got something I got to do."

A bit muzzy from lack of sleep and emotionally overwrought, I answered her mysterious statement with, "Oh? Well, carry on then." I had no idea what that kid was up to. Had I known, I would have, would have…what? Stopped the flow of this wild river?

TWELVE

Destination France

*W*HEN I REGAINED my memory, I also gained a burning desire that fueled new passion and youthful energy in me. That passion was to find *Marie Celine*. More than ever, I felt this fire.

Where to begin? My answer came shortly.

The next day on lunch break, Anne burst into my cabin, breathless with excitement. She took the ship's half model I was carving, and set it gently on the bench. Seizing my hands, she held tightly, as if to keep me from flying away. "Dad, we're finding *Marie Celine*. I have clues! She's alive. I really, really, really, feel this!"

At first I was astonished into silence. Astonished at the very mention of my *Marie Celine*, as I see her, alive…a living spirit. A flicker of hope turned my lips up into a tentative smile. I chanced a shy peek into Anne's face, rosy with zeal, it was. It felt as if I had been hit with a warm, golden glow. Hold it, I told myself. Hold this feeling. She looked back at me expectantly. I opened my mouth to speak and nothing came out. I had to simmer down. Then, "Careful, love. Tell me what has possessed you to make such a statement?"

"Sooo easy, Dad! On the computer, of course. There was this guy who said he was saved by a sailboat? Remember? Slater? He's the key. We're tracking him now."

"Who is we?"

"Oh, chuh, Graydon, of course."

"I see."

"Dad, I'm teaching you the computer! You'll be surfing the 'net, you'll have e-mail."

"I see." As I surveyed the rough-hewn beams of my studio I thought, could it be possible at this time of my life?

Indeed, I was propelled into the world that I had shunned, that queer up-to-date commercial knowingness, the towny culture for which I felt strangeness, the whir and buzz of electronics.

Oh well. Young people know these things. And this is a great deal of good fortune for me.

It didn't take long. With a relentless, stern teacher like Anne, I learned (fast and furious) the miracle of the 'net. It became easy, even fun. Rather a marvelous invention, this internet.

Graydon had given us most of our contacts from his research department. Every spare moment, Anne and I huddled in her cluttered cabin, hovering over the desktop searching for people involved in the evacuation—data from the British archives, and war museums, and groups associated with the Little Ships. We read that Unfound Ships had been discovered around the world in places as far as San Francisco, California, and as close to home as the backwaters of Belfast. Most of the time we hit dead ends—old sites, bounced e-mails, or we were blocked by restricted material. There were some instances where it was required that one be present in England, at the Imperial War Museum, to pore over letters and documents, which of course, was out of the question. We were propelled through our work details at the lodge by the fever of the hunt.

Occasionally the spearhead of fear stabbed me. What if she were dead? At the bottom of the Channel? What if she did live through that horror and was salvaged from a beach for her parts? The thought shriveled me. Late at night, after Anne and I came to a dead end, I would lie awake with these fears. The moon moved by my windows, spilling silver-blue shadows across my bed, and I would see *Marie Celine*, like a ghost ship, sail across these shadow waves, away from me.

Though making little headway, we did not give up. While our bored dogs whined from the fire hearth, Cici entertained guests down at the lodge, and we pressed on.

"The key, Dad, is that English soldier, Slater, in France. The guy who said he was 'saved by a sailboat' on the documentary," Anne said one day while we reviewed segments of the documentary. "We'll find this guy, if he's alive!"

"It appears a bit of a remote chance, Anne. We haven't found anything on him yet." I was dejected at this juncture.

"I've recruited Gidney. We're meeting with him tomorrow at the Village Corner."

"Oh? I see…the village. Go to the town?"

It was a wild ride in our supply van, with Anne driving, playing loud rock on the radio as I attempted to sink into what thoughts I could hear in my head above that awful music.

With my ears ringing, we reached Lunenburg town limits. I always did admire the beauty of this little town. Victorian homes with their ornate trim, and square, sturdy Georgians, all painted in gay colours, stepped down the hillside to the harbour. The harbour dazzled with sunlight. Sailing boats and tall ships out of winter storage were berthed along the waterfront and anchored out in the sheltered waters. The forest of spars made me think of my dad and how this harbour had looked when he was a child.

The Village Corner was the most popular coffee place to go, I was told. The little deck looking over the harbour was jammed with locals drinking coffee, and enjoying the late morning sun and some gossip. What was disturbing about the Corner crowd was the variety of queer looks Anne and I received from the locals. It caused me to inspect my denim shirt and jeans. Had I left breakfast hanging off my collar, egg yolk or something? Anne winked at me knowingly. "You're famous, you know. A lot of people saw the first segment of the series. Ratings are high. I read it this morning on the 'net."

Sitting in the back corner was Graydon, with a bookish bearing in his spectacles and black city clothes. He was engrossed in reading documents and did not notice us until we sat at his table.

Anne said, "Hey Gid. How's it going?"

Graydon stood and shook our hands. "Hey yourself, Anne." Then to me, "Colley?"

"Graydon!" I was pleased to see him.

"I'll get coffees." Anne went into the coffee shop. We settled in our seats. Graydon looked after Anne.

"Well, your daughter is really a different kid from our first meetings."

I followed his gaze as she moved through the crowd like a deer through a thicket. The sun spun her wild hair into silky flaxen threads. I replied, "Oh, well today she is wearing her summer wardrobe, you see. Those black high-top tennis shoes are far more fashionable than the combat boots she wore this past winter. The desert pattern on her fatigues is somewhat more becoming to her complexion than the winter olive-greens, don't you think?"

Graydon let out a short laugh. "Colley, you have to get used to those fashions." He thought a second. "Anne's a little old for the grunge look. She'll grow out of that."

Dubious, I crossed my arms and looked at him.

"We've been in communication since that first night you guys played the documentary. Really, she's motivated. Great kid."

I learned that Graydon had arranged to meet us at the Village Corner, although he did have a meeting back in Halifax. This restricted his time, but he promised that, as soon as he could, he would spend time with us at the lodge.

"Oh, and Colin, I received this e-mail from an old friend of yours, I believe." He handed me the letter off the top of his papers.

I read, "Dear Colley, Elizabeth Whitehead on this end. This is rather a bold obtrusion if you are not Colin Neville of my childhood, who was believed to be lost in the war. If you are indeed our Colley, your father was Dr. Richard Neville. My father was Dr. Angus Whitehead. We were raised together. We spent our holidays at my grandmother Whitehead's farm. You were a cracking good fly fisherman and a brave sailor. Our families were going to sail around the world on your family yacht, *Marie Celine*. If you can recall me, please write…" And she gave her e-mail. I ran my fingers through my hair, staring at the letter. Graydon looked on with open curiosity. "Oh my," I said, "I do know this person."

Anne returned with a tray of coffees and Danish. She read over my shoulder. "You know this lady?"

I reddened. "I rather think I do." I folded the note and put it in my pocket. "Now, let's carry on."

Graydon placed his hands protectively on the pile of papers, fanning out his long, manicured fingers. "I have the information I think you need."

Anne eyed the stack. "Unbelievable, Gid!"

Graydon tightened his grip. "Hold on, Miss Anne. This is valuable material—a lend from a comrade of mine over at BBC, London. It's declassified; however, it's a work in progress by the British government."

I interjected. "Graydon. This is entirely too much trouble for you. Risky. This is valuable material. And to come all this way…"

"Colley, I'm really, really enthused about your venture. I want to be a part of it. To be straight with you, it is a story. But beyond that… well, hell, it's the most fascinating thing I've come across in years! From what Anne and I have deduced, this may be the key to finding the *Marie Celine*…if she is still alive!" He tapped the pile of paperwork firmly with his fingertips.

Graydon went on to explain that he followed Anne's notion that the yacht ended up in France and that the soldier mentioned in the CBC special, Rod Slater, the one who was "saved by a sailboat," had to be a key to the *Marie Celine's* ultimate location. Graydon took it from there, and through research sources in his business and colleagues in England, he obtained a great deal of information. The British documents were a compilation of notes, letters, military reports, interrogations, and investigations from within the Special Operations Executive (SOE) undertakings in France. The SOE was a fresh startup of clandestine and irregular warfare, designed to beat the Germans at subversive activities after Hitler's annexation of Austria in 1938.

"It appears," he said, while carefully pulling out a sheaf marked History, XIII, chapter v, Annex H3, "according to my sources, there was a force in the SOE called 'F Section.' This was made up of the Independent Free French. The British HQ felt that F Section was the most effective in the French Resistance operations. A subgroup of F was DF. DF was in charge of escape routes. DF's operators, it says here," he pulled a report from the sheaf, "lived in hourly peril of their lives. Their task was to provide clandestine communications to and from Western Europe by sea and land, principally to run escape lines across, from, or around France into the Iberian and Breton peninsulas. Several hundred passengers were carried by sea and none of them were lost, and the carriers' casualty rate of two percent," he read, "was by far the lowest of the sections we are concerned with. This DF group provided safe houses, clothes and forged documents. From sea, DF kept the allies informed of enemy activity on beaches and on the water. They also provided communications needed for smuggling agents and refugees out of France."

"Wow!" Anne gleamed. "Those DF guys were real heroes."

"And," Graydon was surely enjoying this venture, "the section head of the field in the south, was a young staff officer stationed in southern France. Major Rod Slater, code name 'Pug.' He was one of the first, and youngest, agents to parachute into occupied France through the fuselage floor of a Whitley."

"I say, Graydon, I do think he could be the one mentioned in your special."

"Strong probability, Colin. Strong. However, there may be difficulties."

"How come? We got the secret files." Anne was leaning forward on the table, fizzing.

"For one," Graydon studied a page of the report, "the agents in the field had several names. They had a secret name for 10 Downing, another secret name for Whitehall…the code name. And another field name on the forged papers."

We huddled close round Graydon as he picked through the pile. "I've not read all the papers yet. But I thought I had a…ah-ha! I knew this one was in here. It's a segment of his PF—personal file, to you guys. Here, yes! He married one of his DF agents. A French agent, code name of Mimi. Civilian name, Jeanine Cormeau. Born and raised in the village of Valras, Languadoc, southern France. She and her mother ran a safe house there. Close to the beaches. Of course, evacuees would be picked up from a beach."

We nodded with mounting enthusiasm. He snatched a stray paper falling to the ground like a portentous feather floating from the sky. Graydon glanced at it, then focused again with greater interest. He frowned. Anne and I waited.

Reading it, Graydon said, "It's a decoded teleprint from Major Rod Slater's PF." He read aloud:

TPR 1028   12th March 1943

BLUFF CHECK OMITTED   TRUE CHECK OMITTED

FOLLOWING NEWS FROM MARSEILLES STOP PUG DISAPPEARED BELIEVED TO BE ARRESTED BY GESTAPO STOP BELIEVED EXECUTED STOP SECOND RADIO OPERATOR SUSPECTED STOP DO NOT SEND HIM FOR PICK UP STOP BELIEVE ARRESTATION IS DUE TO THIS OPERATOR STOP SUSPECTED HE IS THE COMMUNIST SECTION THIEF WHO GAVE ADDRESSES ADIEU

Graydon put the message carefully back in the folder. He took off his glasses and rubbed his eyes, blinked them clear a few times and replaced the glasses. He crossed his arms over the folders and stared at the tabletop. "I don't know where to go from here. I hadn't seen that paper till now."

"Damn!" I felt that life was once again ebbing from me, leaving me behind on a deserted beach.

"What now?" Anne slumped across the table, chin resting on her fists. "This is the shits."

On the way back home, my head resting against the passenger window, I followed the lobster boats putting in the bay. Our one lead to the mystery of *Marie Celine* had died with Rod Slater. I concluded that I was quite a bit happier before I regained my memory. With my brain highways all cleared of roadblocks, suddenly I felt raw. This effusive being, this whole self for which I had longed, was no longer a dim dream. And here came, rolling and tumbling over me, a new bundle, chock-full of feelings. With this new expansiveness, I experienced intense love, hope, loss, disappointment, anger, fear. At once, it was too much. Perhaps I should have been left alone back in my naked, simple life, watching silver-white clouds lancing a sapphire-blue sky.

I leaned my head against the window, sighed and slid down in my seat. Anne gave me an astonished grin. "Dad, you look miserable!"

Not amused, I raised my brows at her and fixed my eyes on the road ahead. A few images of Elizabeth Whitehead flickered through my vision. That beautiful child with the horses. I would write her, of course, but what, oh, what to say? Was she married? What was she like…?

We drove on along the Point Road hoping to catch the ferry. Anne's rock music crashed in my sensitive ears. Then, abruptly, she switched off the music. "Dad, I'm going to France."

"Oh, no. You're not going abroad."

"Oh yeah, I am."

This was mutiny. "You need to be home. You said you would never go to France, after the French nuns from Quebec gave you a rough time."

"I'm on a fact-finding mission, not a diplomatic mission. So what if they're gross and eat gross foods? And always think they're right."

"You flunked out of French in school, young lady."

Anne jutted her chin out and lifted her head high and looked down her nose at the road. "I can speak perfect French. Parisian French… when I want to."

"Oh, no, no, no." I did not think that my child was ready for the world. "We won't give you money. We can't afford anything like that!"

"You forgot my trust fund."

"That's for college. And well…emergencies." I was sure I had won this one.

"I don't want to go to college. Ever again. And this is an emergency! And Dad, I am of age now to receive my fund payments."

"You're not going abroad, and that is my final word!" I grunted and growled, crossed my arms, and was effectively tough.

Not long after that, Cici saw Anne off on a flight from Halifax. From there she was bound for London, to Air France, to Charles De Gaulle, to Marseilles.

I was told this, for I would not come out of my cabin. I listened to Ralph Vaughn William's *The Lark Ascending* and mourned the loss of hope of finding *Marie Celine*. The loss of a life nearly gained. It may have been better to never know than to have Anne discover that my *Marie Celine* was, indeed, lost forever.

* * * *

Cici and I took watches on the computer in Anne's cabin, awaiting news from Anne. She had got a new laptop for her trip. Neophytes that we were, there was a lot of time taken learning how to work these machines. At first we lost a lot of information. It didn't take long, however, for Anne to realize our difficulty, and she re-sent her letters, with instructions on how to save them and how not to delete them. We had so many e-mails from her that Cici invested in a second and bigger computer that we put into the pastry room off the kitchen. I also secretly waited for a reply from my lost love, Lizbeth. I had sent off a short note to her, very formal, affirming that I was her "Colley." I stole into the pantry before Cici, to scroll down the e-mails. No word from Lizbeth. Anne? We had torrents of news. Our lives were full of the search for *Marie Celine*.

THIRTEEN

Anne's Story

ANNE ARRIVED IN the fishing village of Valras, where the war documents had indicated Rod Slater could have been living. He had married a local girl, Jeanine. If he were alive, Anne was sure that he would still be in this region. It was a holiday weekend and she dragged her luggage, mostly filled with copies of the documents from the war archives, through the streets of this Mediterranean town looking for a hotel. She took in the town, the sandstone, the white-washed buildings with red-tiled roofs, the narrow cobbled lanes leading to the beaches, where the sea was truly azure blue, dappled with silver coins of sunshine. The main streets were lined with sidewalk cafes, the patios bustled with people, and wild gypsy-looking fabrics hung from the eaves of shops. It was so different from home, where the sea was grey-green, lined with black rocks, and dark green forests of pine, spruce, maple, tamarack, and birch; colours were more orderly, muted. She really did not know what to think. After all, she had never been out of Nova Scotia and she was already feeling homesick.

Her high-topped Keds were hurting her feet. She was hungry, having eaten nothing but a bit of bread and tea on the trip. She was too nervous to eat. And anyway, she could not really understand the French terms for food on the menus. Food terms were different from the French in school, she reasoned.

She finally found a little stone hotel off the main street, "Hotel Riquet." The interior was cave-like, dark with stone and plaster walls, low ceilings with age-darkened beams, and all the doorways were arched. The girl at the desk gave her a big shrug and pretended not to understand her college French. Anne was wilted with fatigue, becoming discouraged and a little desperate. She tried again to communicate with the obstinate desk girl, who rolled her eyes and gave another shrug. At that moment a man appeared at her side. Anne thought he looked like Salvador Dali, with plastered-down hair, dyed jet-black, the Dali mustache, and a formal black suit with a bow tie. He said, in perfect English, "Are you English?"

Anne said, "No, Canadian." And he brightened.

"Ah good! I do not like the English. I love the Canadians. But of course, we have one room left. Just for you! I am Monsieur Riquet!" He kissed her hand. Anne pursed her lips.

But of course, she took the room. It was tiny and on the third floor. It was done in post-war modern plastic and lacquer décor. It sported a small window that looked down on a skylight over the kitchen at the café across the alley. She could not open the bathroom door all the way as it hit the foot of the bed. After she wedged her way in, she found it was the size of an airplane bathroom and just as utilitarian. Except for one luxury piece: a spigot in the wall by the mini sink that was labelled Cotes D'Or, vin rouge. She tried it and stared: red wine really did come out.

Feeling very homesick, she flopped into bed and slept a long time.

The trash truck woke her the next morning. The smells of roasting coffee beans and baking bread drifted through her window from the café below. She first went to the dining room at the hotel and found it brimming with noisy guests, so she ended up at the café across the alley. Chez Louis's had a little wooden fence facing the main street; empty chairs and tables stood waiting for customers to arrive. Anne noted with a chuckle that Christmas lights still hung around the exterior. She loved the inside because it felt more like home. It was wood and stone with oak rafters and beams. Copper pots hung everywhere. Long wooden tables and benches stretched across the back. A long nickel bar guarded the open kitchen beyond.

This morning, the bar was packed with men standing shoulder-to-shoulder, drinking coffee or tumblers of red wine. It seemed to be a real local place. Some of the men were dressed in light linen or cotton summer suits; others wore khaki work clothes. There was a low hum of baritone, almost musical, male voices.

Serving the bar were two men in long white aprons. One was young, dark, a good-looker, and she figured near her age. The other fellow, Anne noted, was really old. He was tall and bent over with long grey hair that was fuzzy, like cotton candy. There was something loveable about him, she thought, like a little kid who had just gotten out of bed. His eyes had smiley wrinkles with bags underneath. He was at the far end of the bar smoking a cigarette and drinking a bowl of coffee. The younger one was drinking red wine from a tumbler.

Anne moved up to the bar and edged her way to the far end. No one noticed her; she felt invisible. It was an uncomfortable feeling. In a moment, the old man saw her and bumped the younger man, upsetting his glass of wine. The young one paused, focusing on Anne in a curious manner. She found her hand edged up to pat down her hair. She stole a glance at her British desert-khaki fatigues from her favourite mail-order shop, India Company. Her jacket was unbuttoned just enough to show off her genuine British military singlet. Suddenly she felt displaced.

He gave an insolent half-smile, moved down the bar and said, "*Mademoiselle?*"

Anne noticed his face was tan and smooth, but for the new growth of black stubble. His hair, she thought, was blue-black, like a blackbird's—thick, straight, and longish.

Anne could not think of a French word for decaf. So she simply said, "Decaf."

He gave a pompous sniff, "Ah, *non*."

"Herb tea?" she asked, in her best Parisian French.

"Ah, *non*."

"Green tea?"

"Ah, *non*."

Anne gave up. "Coffee?"

"Ah, *oui*."

His direct look made her nervous, and she forgot how to say, "Plain. Black. Coffee." She tried a few words. He raised his brows and turned to the big brass machine. He returned with a messy, dripping cup of boiled cream blended with coffee. She was annoyed. Most of this mess was in the saucer. She asked in her best French for a *serviette*. He gave her a look. The men at the bar hushed and watched her, amused. Then, the waiter announced to the bar, "Ah, *serrr—vi—yet-tah*!" Anne did not get it. He rolled his R's and made the end of the word sound as if it ended in "A". She did not think the word ended in an "A". He did return with a large white napkin and, with brisk formality, folded it and slid it by her saucer.

The decibel of men's voices once more rose to a low roar. The waiter moved back down the bar. Dabbing cream off her saucer, Anne called after him, in French, asking him if he knew of a Slater family in the area and if so, where did they live.

The bar went quiet. The old man and the young man conferred in whispers. The older man went over to Anne. "My name is Louis Mourier." He held out his hand.

Anne shook his hand. "Anne Neville".

"Neville? Ah, Neville." His eyes blinked with ambiguous recognition. He recovered quickly. "English? Then you are English."

Anne sighed. "No, Canadian." Then she repeated her question in French.

Louis smiled politely and gave an apologetic shrug. The young man came to his side and said with frosty formality, "Please speak English." His tanned, boyish face was stiff with an expression like an ice wall.

Anne repeated in the stilted English that people use when they are trying to talk to foreigners. "Rod Slater? Know Rod Slater? Englishman? Famous resistance fighter, here in southern France." She pointed her finger to the floor, "Here" and gesticulated, as if she were in a pow-wow in an old western movie, arms waving, speaking in monosyllables. "Wife. French. Jeanine? Cormeau? Family lived here."

The group went stony-faced. Finally, Younger Man said, "Why are you seeking this person in our village?"

"Rod Slater knows my family's boat, *Marie Celine*. I am looking for the sailboat called *Marie Celine*."

He considered her briefly then held up his hands in a dismissive manner and said, "I am so sorry. We cannot help you. Perhaps another village."

The men at the bar turned their backs to her, and Louis and Younger Man returned to their posts, busy with wiping counters. Younger Man was lying, she could tell. Without touching her coffee, she put her money on the counter, "That's fine. Thanks. I'll look him up on the 'net." Reaching the patio, she heard a roar of men's voices mimicking her. More laughter.

Anne had a bad feeling that she was not going to find out anything about Slater, alive or dead. Back at the hotel desk she looked through different phone books and a computerized directory at the desk. She felt so close being in the region where all the resistance activity with Slater occurred, and yet there was not a clue in the local directories.

M. Riquet came up beside her. "Can I help with anything? You look anxious."

She told him that she was looking for the Slaters or anyone related. In an instant he drew a map. "His name is not in the books, but his vineyard and winery are listed. But of course, how would you know? He is English, but more like French now. A local hero, you know. Very brave man. The house is not far. Just up the river."

Anne rented a bicycle from M. Riquet and rode up the River Orb along the D19 to the D64, through vineyards and delta. With every push of the pedals she exclaimed, "He's alive! Alive!" She found the Slater house set back off the road in a vineyard. There were plane trees and ancient, moss-covered stone walls around the light-yellow sandstone house. There were a large porch and a heavy arched wooden door. Like a monastery door, Anne thought. The stone walkway made its way through a tangled, over-grown garden of English thyme with blue and white flowers, purple and white lavender bushes, trellised berries, and patches of summer vegetables.

Anne leaned her bike against the wall by the gate and stood there in a panic. Her chest felt tight. She thought of all the people who had lived because of *Marie Celine*. She could not even fathom time, the war. It was a different world to her. And yet, she felt that time in history was becoming part of her. She let herself through the wooden gate, climbed the stone steps and knocked on the heavy door.

Rubbing her knuckles, Anne was startled by the heavy door creaking open a slit. A woman's face could be seen. A tanned, tight-skinned face, soft chestnut eyes, high cheekbones, and grey hair pulled back and tucked in a paisley bandana. She still had the features of the photo Anne had in her backpack of a young, beautiful Jeanine Cormeau, Agent Mimi, Free French Resistance.

"Madame Slater?"

"*Oui?*" She said this so softly, it was like a sigh. Anne was not sure Jeanine heard her. Anne then introduced herself, in French, and told her that it was very important that she speak with Madame. She asked her if she were the wife of Major Rod Slater of Free French Resistance and the Agent for the Special Operations Executive, in England.

Shunning, Jeanine shook her head, and the cast-iron latch clicked as the door was shut in Anne's face. She was mortified. Had she frightened this woman? Did Rod Slater exist? Didn't Riquet say he was alive? Or did he? Rod Slater was the only hope for finding *Marie*. Dejected and confused, Anne was turning to leave when she heard hurried footsteps on stone floors within, and muffled voices. And the door swung open.

FOURTEEN

Major Rod Slater Found

AT FIRST GLANCE, Anne thought Major Rod Slater looked fierce. He was tall and sturdy. Pretty bald. Not one ounce of fat or loose skin. His face was a fighter's face, pushed-in, blunt, scarred, as if he had been caught in a buzz saw. His mouth was stern, marked with deep creases. His right hand was paw-like and his other hand was missing; there was a stump where a hand should have been. With a soft, but gruff voice, and with a British accent, he commanded, "Lass, I think you'd better be coming in."

After introductions, Anne followed Slater across worn stone floors and down a hall, past a formal parlour to a stone and plaster kitchen in the rear of the house. It had high-beamed ceilings, deep-set paned windows with potted pink, white, and red geraniums on the sills.

Outside the windows, lush vineyards with multicoloured roses heading the rows glimmered in the southern sun. Jeanine Slater, slender in long denim skirt and white T-shirt, tapped in clogs over the floor tending a gas stovetop that had been retrofitted into an ancient stone hearth. She poured water over rough-ground coffee in an enamel pot. Rod introduced Anne. Very serious, she inclined her head and resumed her work.

Anne was seated at a worn pine table. Rod sat opposite. He took a long deep breath. "Miss, ah, Neville. You're not from the old country are you?"

Anne shook her head.

"Yank?" he asked.

"Canadian," she told him.

"What do you want with us?"

Anne studied his frank open face and shot right out, "You know about a sailboat, *Marie Celine*. You said that you were saved by her."

He said, "Our Angel Ship? Our *Marie?*" Rod exchanged a wary look with Jeanine.

"Your ship?" Anne challenged.

"She saved me. Yes. She saved all of us that morning on the beaches of Dunkirk. She lifted us from hell. Then during the war, she saved refugees, prisoners of war, agents of the French Resistance. Yes, our angel. All of us who survived the war." He paused and shook his head abruptly, as if banishing an unwanted vision. "Your name is Neville. You are related to this boat somehow. Canada?"

"My father," Anne said. Rod stared, perplexed.

Anne explained, "Married late in life. He's Canadian, but born in Britain. My grandfather built that boat. My father sailed in *Marie Celine* with his parents to evacuate the British forces off the beaches of Dunkirk." She could tell by the fizzing in the atmosphere, by the audible sucking in of breath, that something was up.

Jeanine placed the coffee, steamed cream, bread, and a crock of honey on the table. She poured coffee and cream in each bowl and sat beside Anne. Something about her settled, calm confidence helped Anne feel better. And for the first time in her life, Anne liked coffee. She thought it tasted of nuts, caramel, vanilla.

Rod said, "You are aware, Miss Neville, we do not know yet if this is the same boat. Can you give us more background? Details?"

Anne recounted the story of her dad, up to the BBC series and the return of his memory. The Slaters listened, entranced. When Anne was finished, Rod said, "That bit about your father's boat sailing herself away? This could be how she arrived on our beach. You see, we were left. Abandoned."

Rod told Anne the story of himself, Captain Pierre Jeantot, and the remainder of his French army unit: Eric Trubert, Louis Mourier, and Paco Torres. He told of their incredible journey on the *Marie Celine*, home to Valras. He told Anne of the boat's life as a secret agent boat and of the first covert journey. "That first night in *Marie Celine*, we met the felucca offshore." He saw the question in Anne's face. "Feluccas are a type of boat seen everywhere in the Mediterranean. They have been used for fishing and freight since the days of ancient Egypt, when they were sailed on the Nile. Such a common boat was the perfect craft for transporting our people out of France. The agents, crewing this felucca, crazy Polish, were recklessly brave. Too rough even for the Polish navy. They picked me up and got me to a British transport ship and that got me back to England.

"In hospital, they operated on me a few times. Every day these officers came to my bed and debriefed me. These men were agents of the Special Operations Executive—the S-O-E.

"When I was good as new, they enlisted me into service with the SOE. I trained daily in the French language and in operating, dismantling, and repairing the wireless. They taught me code, navigation, and covert sea operations. It was all hush-hush.

"We stayed in different specialized camps throughout rural England. I had three different names: one for Baker Street offices, one for Whitehall offices, and one for field offices. It was just as well. My future job in the SOE, in France, would be very dangerous.

"I was head of the DF unit, which was the SOE escape section. We were the people who organized clothing, forged papers and ration tickets for agents and refugees. As head of the DF unit, it was my responsibility to arrange escape lines for agents and refugees either over the

Pyrenees by foot, or picked up in rural fields by plane—or by boats off the beaches. I can assure you that Angel Ship saved the lives of many people. She took them home to safety. She helped freedom survive.

"She was also an offshore monitor, sending back information on enemy activity in our part of the Mediterranean, to enable pick-ups and transport of agents and refugees. This Angel Ship is a hero." Anne noted that Rod said that last bit in the present tense. And, she thought for the first time, that *Marie* could be alive.

He pulled his sleeve over his stump and studied the table. "Then, one of my radio operators turned me in."

Stunned, Anne realized that she had read about that arrest in the papers that Graydon had provided. "Dad and I read that you were turned in. And executed! Who? How? Why, we thought you were dead!"

Rod grimaced, remembering. "One man in our crew coming home from Dunkirk, Sergeant Paco Torres, left us as soon as we arrived in Valras. He was Pierre's best worker in the boatyard. We heard he was with relatives in Barcelona. One day he came back and asked to be a part of our Free French Resistance team. I taught him how to use the wireless. He was very good. One night, I was called to a meeting near Marseilles. There, the Nazis arrested me and the other agents. Only Paco and Jeanine's mother, Agent Cormeau, knew of that meeting.

"The Germans tortured me—cut off my hand—but they did not get any information. They took my group and me to a pit and shot us. Somehow I was not hit. I fell back into the pit.

"That night I crawled out of the death pit and walked behind enemy lines for days to get home. When I arrived here, everything was gone. Paco Torres had informed on Agent Cormeau. She was arrested. The Cormeau family home burned. My resistance group had all disappeared into hiding along with Jeanine, who was called Agent Mimi." Rod let out a pained wheeze. "Jeanine's mum was shot in the camp.

"It turned out Paco was a communist. He went with the Nazis hoping they would rule France after the war. They felt that the British and French resistance fighters' attempt to keep up the war against the Nazis was a capitalist plot, pushed by greed and profit. Later, that all changed when the Nazis invaded Russia. But, the communists were fanatical and dangerous. Still are. And Paco is a fugitive, wanted for collaborating with the Nazis. I heard he is now a communist agitator in Catalonia. A crazed extremist."

Jeanine reached across the table and put her hand over Rod's and they sat there a long time looking into each other's eyes. Anne felt a mixture of pain, confusion, and wonder.

Before Anne could ask what happened, some vineyard workers came to the back porch.

Rod met them at the door. There were heated words, and he came back. "Look lass, Jeanine and I have to go settle a row going on here. We have a lot more to talk about. Why don't you come for supper tonight?" They both stood. "Yes, please," Jeanine pressed.

"I'd love to…" Anne started, but had to shoot out her desperate questions. "But, look, I have to know, is the boat alive? Can I see her? Where is she?"

They looked at each other. Finally, Rod said, "Do you promise to do nothing until I can guide you?"

She nodded earnestly.

Finally, Rod admitted, "Yes. She is alive. Here in Valras, at the old boatyard. Not in good shape, I have to admit. Lass, you can't go there until I've cleared it with the others. Especially Pierre Jeantot. He's a very, ah, difficult old cock. You must be sure to stay away from there.

"Don't speak of our conversation with anyone. Also very important: never mention the Resistance in this town. Do you promise to wait for us to help you? Not to take this into your own hands?"

"I promise," Anne said. She felt her mouth go dry. She liked the Slaters a lot. They were exceptional people. But she could not have waited another second. The drive to find the boat was too strong. Suddenly, to her it was the most compelling matter in her life.

Down the road, Anne asked a few truck drivers hanging around the vineyards where the old boatyard was. She pedalled off the main road to a dirt road that ran along the river. She pedalled through golden clouds of insects buzzing in the afternoon sunglow. The grasses smelled like oat hay. And beyond, she could smell the sea-weedy, salty scent of the sea. Much different sea and smells than home.

Anne went along the back stonewalls of an old commercial complex. She laid her bike in the grass and went in an open side gate. The boatyard was built around a natural basin, and a rock jetty protected it from the river. The yard looked deserted, like a spaceship had come down and beamed everybody up mid-work. A fishing boat, its wood painted in swirls of faded yellows, ochres, and blues, rested in the greyed wooden cradle of the ways; the boat's bottom paint cracking. Scrapers, brushes, files, reefing irons, and other tools she didn't recognize were left rusting on the cobblestones. It was a spooky place. No one was around. No one had been around. It looked as if no one was going to be coming back.

She crept around the shabby wooden workshops and peeked through dirty windows.

There sat idle wood planes, jigsaws, table saws, band saws—all the equipment she had grown up with in her father's shop.

At the end of the yard was a bigger stone and wood building, the windows opaque with years of salt, wind and dust. Part of the foundation was in the river basin. Stone stairs went from a side door down to the water. A concrete ramp with rail tracks went from the deeper part of the basin up to barn-type doors at the front. Anne shivered. She thought she heard a man's voice, above her, coming from the boathouse. She couldn't make out what it said. It was like when one has a dream and someone in the dream is calling. She climbed the stairs.

The stone steps were polished and grooved from years of use. They weren't dusty like everything else around the creepy place. She knocked on the side door, listened, and tried the iron latch. It opened. She stepped on to a mezzanine that bordered the perimeter of the building. It was hard to see, having come in from the sun's glare. Shafts of dim rays shone through the cloudy windows down on the cabin top and decks of a sailboat. She found a stairway to the main room. When she reached the bottom of the stairs, she noticed not only workbenches, but a sitting area, with rickety chairs around a long table topped with empty wine bottles and dirty glasses, filled ashtrays, stale bread, a lamp, and journals, or log-type books. Sitting in her slipway cradle, looking over this party of ghosts was the boat. Anne stood back a bit and looked up at her. There was no doubt about it. After all her life of seeing her lines drawn, her half-hulls and models carved, she was looking at the *Marie Celine.*

Another set of stairs on wheels butted up against the after part of her hull. Anne climbed to the wooden rails, dulled and cracked from lack of varnish, and stepped across wood-planked decks. The planks were sprung from neglect and lack of moisture. Anne's Keds left perfect imprints in the dust. The main hatch doors were open and all she had to do was slide the top of the hatch back. She peered below, down oak steps, into the galley area, and headed down the steps.

It looked like an abandoned castle! There was carved wood every-where; carved beams, all dull, cracking varnish. Raised panels of what looked like mahogany. There was a coal cook stove to the left, iron with nickel trim. There was a sink near the steps and beautifully crafted wood cupboards. And Dutch tiles. Delft tiles. Pretty, in blue and white. The same tiles were on the splash boards and backing for the iron stove. Next, there was an area with a chart table. All around that little alcove were shelves of mouldy books. Past that, was the main saloon area. In the dinette was a wooden dining table and a booth of old, torn, mildewed material. On the other side were settees, in the same old ma-terial, and a tile fireplace. The *Marie* looked pretty beat up. Still, Anne clearly understood the wonder of this ship. It was a mark of accom-plishment, a finished dream, alive and real. It felt as if *Marie* had a soul.

Anne had a list of things to find that would present proof that the boat was, indeed, *Marie.* First she must find what used to be her father's bedroom, to look for a secret box hidden there. She was heading for-ward when she heard a noise from above.

From the hatch, a deep voice jarred her. In flexible, lilting French the deep voice said, "What are you doing here?"

Anne faltered. Then, planting hands firmly on hips, thrusting chin to the ceiling, she turned and said very carefully, in her best French, that this was her father's boat.

Slipping down the companionway steps, he leaned back against the cook stove, arms crossed over a black T-shirt that had GAP lettered across the chest. Baggy shorts, tanned legs, and scuffed boat loafers without socks. It was the younger waiter from Chez Louis.

He raised his thick black brows and rolled his eyes to the cabin ceiling. "Please, Mademoiselle, speak English."

Anne blurted, "This boat's my dad's boat. I have every right to be here."

"Ah. I am sorry," he said flatly, "but you are mistaken. This is my grandfather's boat. Captain Pierre Jeantot, owner of this boatyard. Owner of this boat."

"Well then, your granddad stole my dad's boat!"

He straightened. His dark, amused eyes checked her out from foot to head. Then they heard the sirens. Like those sirens in old English movies—high-low, high-low, whine-whine, coming closer. He leapt across the boat and grabbed Anne's arm, nearly pulling it out of the socket, "Grandfather called the police. Come! Now! They are after you."

Anne balked. "But I didn't do anything."

He twirled her around to the companionway and herded her up the steps. "You do not have to do anything. My grandfather is a very powerful man in this village. At any rate, you did break and enter."

"No way I did. Everything was open!"

"Never mind! Go faster!" he said. "Off the boat."

She reached the deck and monkey-climbed down the metal steps to the floor; he was right behind.

"They're at the entrance of the yard!" He scanned each exit. A second double barn door was at the rear of the building; it was barred with wood planks held by iron L-brackets. Beside that was a small door.

"This door. It goes to the road behind." The sirens were closer. The two of them ran across the boathouse, unlocked the door and were out into bushes that had grown over the unused exit. The waiter shut the door and flattened himself against the wall, pulling Anne with him, snagging in the bush and tamarack trees lining the back wall of the boathouse.

Up the dirt road they saw police cars turning into the main gates of the boatyard. As the last police car zoomed inside the gates, they ran back along the dirt road to a beat-up flatbed lorry that had a Mercedes emblem on the stubby hood. He opened the passenger side and rushed her in. "Not on the seat! On the floor!"

"My bicycle! In the bush, there!"

With an irritated sigh, he ran back and got the bicycle from the bushes and threw it into the bed of the lorry.

They skidded and bounded over ruts and potholes, back along the river. Anne was slammed from seat base to dashboard.

"What is your proper name?" he asked. Dust rose from the cracks in the floorboards.

"Anne Neville. Yours?"

"Alain. Alain Jeantot."

"Can I get up now, Alain? My eyes are filled with dirt."

All she could see was the fine line of his bottom jaw, his black T-shirt billowing in the wind from open windows, and legs so tanned, the dark hairs were golden fur. His head turned towards the side mirrors and he inspected the rear mirror a time, then, "Yes. You can sit. But keep low."

"Where are we going?"

"To your hotel. By the back streets."

She plopped up on the seat and scooted low, holding on to seat and door. "And, by the way, my grandfather built that boat."

He raised his brows. "Your grandfather?" He turned down a short street and jumped across the tourist traffic on the main drag. "Some of the best work I have seen." He said this to himself as he cut another corner coming up on the side of her hotel.

"*Merde*," Alain said, frowning. In front of the hotel, a police car sat straddling the curb; an officer was leaning on the hood, smoking a cigarette. Flanking him were M. Riquet and a grey-haired old man with a short-cropped white beard. The old man had a big paunch and bowed legs. He was wearing baggy suit pants, held up with old-time suspenders, and a white dress shirt with round collar. He was ranting and waving his arms at M. Riquet, who was just as animated.

"Hum. Grandfather. We go!" Alain backed the lorry into an alley and peeled out away from the hotel, cutting a corner off a park where men were playing Petanque. They shook their fists and yelled.

"That's your grandfather?"

"Ah, yes." He concentrated on speeding out of town.

"He looks—like totally ferocious."

"Formidable. Terrible. You do not want to meet with him. It is best you leave town."

"Uh-uh."

He looked at her a second with insolent eyes. "Ah, yes. You will go."

"Hey, then why did you help me anyway?"

"I thought about letting you get arrested. You see, I told Grandfather of your questions about the boat when you came into Chez Louis."

"Rat!"

"Then, I realized, if you were arrested, the Canadians come, the English come. There is an international incident. The ownership of the boat will be questioned. There will be another world war in our village. The French hate the English and the English hate the French! Just like that." He cut the air with his hand, then he pointed to the sky, "This I know is true. I do not want this problem, for someday that boat will be mine."

"Not!"

"Oh, yes. This I want. And this I will get. And, therefore, you must leave France. Forget this impossible mission."

Anne decided that he sounded like a self-indulgent spoiled brat. She replied, "In your dreams." Anne was used to getting her way at home.

She steamed; there was no way in hell that guy was getting that boat. Alain pulled up by Rod and Jeanine's vineyard and slowed down.

Anne was shaken. "I can't go to the Slaters'."

He raised his brows and said dryly, "And why not? We must keep you out of sight for a time. You imposed upon them earlier today. This I know."

"No, please. I can't. I feel like a shit." Alain leaned on the steering wheel and measured her with a shrewd, but not unfriendly, gaze. She admitted, sputtering in staccato, "Look. I did intrude. That was rude. Then they were so nice. I felt really good about them. And I promised I wouldn't go to the boat until Rod had a meeting with everyone involved. I blew it."

Alain nodded, knowingly, "Yes, you did." He put the flatbed in gear and drove up the driveway. "We go to the Slaters'."

Pausing near the garden area by the front gate, Alain rushed Anne out of the cab and set the bike off to the side of the road. Rod, in the garden, happened to notice them and began to gesture. Alain shook his head and waved out the window as he backed down the drive in a whirl of dust.

Anne was upset. About everything. And now she had to face Rod, who was standing there waving her in. "Hullo, Miss Neville." Rod's cheeriness was encouraging.

Anne followed Rod back to the kitchen. They were joined by Jeanine, who gave Anne a hug and a kiss on one cheek. She stood at the sink and asked her husband, "Was that Alain just now?"

"Yes, love."

"Why didn't he stay?"

"Who knows? Perhaps he is late for his job. You know, his job as The-Waiter-Who-Insults-The-Customers?" He chuckled. Jeanine laughed.

Rod seated Anne at the table and slid his large frame into the chair across from her. This homey feeling made her burn hot with guilt about the deception that afternoon. For sure they would hear from Captain Pierre shortly. She picked at the seafood stew Jeanine put before her.

Rod took over. "Lass, you'll starve here in France for God's sake.

Looks like you could use a little meat on your bones. Muscle for your quest. You'd better clean your plate. And by the by, we know about your 'break and entering' this afternoon." He chuckled. Anne's face seared with embarrassment.

"Oh," she murmured. Rod and Jeanine gave her a stern look.

"I want the rest of the story. How did you end up with Alain-the-Disinherited? Pierre didn't know how you got away."

She told him how Alain had busted her in the saloon of *Marie*, and of the escape to the hotel, and the rerouting to their house.

"What's with Alain?" Anne asked.

Rod said, "We know he's not living with his grandfather anymore, and the boatyard's gone to hell. I believe that Jose Ignacio Torres—that's Paco's nephew—and Alain got into a row. Jose Ignacio and his whole family quit the boatyard. Pierre fired Alain and cut off his allowance. We don't know what's going on now. All of the Torres family is from Catalonia. These Catalans have worked in that yard for generations. I think they left France."

Jeanine had a knowing glow in her eyes. She said to Rod. "Oh, I think Alain's sleeping at Louis's place."

Rod winced. "That boy's a natural at woodmanship." Rod added, "A rare talent, needed with classic boats. He lived to mess about with *Marie*. When he was a kid, after school, he'd be allowed a short time on her. He attached himself to that boat. Over the years, we didn't have the money to keep her up. Alain tried, but between work apprenticeships in England, and school, he didn't have time any more. Then he was banished from the boat and the boatyard. We, the original crew for *Marie*, we couldn't keep up the boat." He broke off and swirled his wineglass, watching the rosé reflectively.

Anne said, "You guys, Alain told me he was going to own *Marie Celine*. I'm not letting him take my dad's life away from him. Not now. Dad just got a second chance."

Rod frowned. "You saw the boat. How do you know for certain that's the one?"

She told him of the years of seeing models in the workshop. She told Rod and Jeanine how she had lists of clues to search for in the boat, such as, where the documentation numbers should have been carved in a structural part of the boat. She was to look for those numbers. Then, the secret hiding place of the childhood treasures; she did not tell Rod where they had been hidden.

Rod appeared uncomfortable. He cleared his throat, "The boat's numbers were covered. There had been some damage. It was to our advantage to cover them in case of boarding by Germans. Any boat, save English or French, may have been left alone. As for your father's treasures, I know where they are, and I am quite sure that Pierre has forgotten everything about them. The only time he took a look at them, we came under attack by enemy craft. They've been hidden since then…almost sixty years, unless Alain found the cache. I reckon we'd better clear this up. We'll have to go to the boatyard."

The three of them jammed into Jeanine's Renault and careened along the back roads to the boatyard. The main gate was open. They swung in and nearly rammed the back end of a lorry. It was long, rusty and dented, with a flatbed that was only inches off the ground. Rod punched down the brakes. "Shit. That lorry's meant to move a boat. Bloody hell." He maneuvered around the truck and rumbled over the cobblestones to the back of the yard. The boathouse doors were open and they saw *Marie Celine's* fine stern edging out, suspended over the water. Long manila lines were attached to her, held by unseen hands inside the boathouse. "Get moving!" Rod was out of the car in a flash, with Anne and Jeanine at his heels.

At that moment, Alain's truck skidded up.

They had reached the side door and ran up along the mezzanine. Down in the boathouse were Eric and Louis holding long lines attached to the boat, with Pierre on the winch brake.

Alain was the first one down to the main floor. He sprinted for Pierre and grabbed the brake, trying to stop the carriage. The other men dropped their lines and hurried to stop him. They wrestled with Alain, pushing him off the brake. With the brake released, the carriage took off down the rail track. Wedges fell away from the hull. There was a scramble for lines. Alain grabbed the brake handle again, and the cradle started to slow, but there was too much momentum now. *Marie*, freed by the loosened wedges, slid stern first into the water. Her weight at impact caused a wake that momentarily buried her stern. For a second, she looked as if she had reared up on her transom and was going to hurl out of the water like a lance. Instead she wavered, hobby-horsed and came down hard on her bow. They all heard the crack as her bow hit supporting timbers of the cradle. Alain yelled at Pierre, "If that is the stem that broke, so help me Grandfather, I will never, never forgive you!"

The boathouse went quiet, the men frozen in place, as if the music to this savage dance had abruptly stopped. They exchanged dumb, blank looks. A second passed before they snapped out of it and scrambled to save her.

Jeanine and Anne ran outside and down along the pier on the port side of *Marie*. From the opposite pier, Alain jumped on the boat and tossed Jeanine and Anne the lines. They missed. The ropes sank into the water. Ebbing tidal flow tugged and tried to suck *Marie* away. Alain retrieved the lines and heaved again. After a few tries, Anne and Jeanine caught them.

"Give a turn around those cleats," he commanded. "Fast! Throw a loop over one end of the cleat. Understand?" They did. They cleated off the boat and held her steady.

Inside, they heard the whine and chug of the winch as it started up, ready to pull the cradle up the tracks. *Marie*, floating now, graceful and subdued, became easy to handle. But they had to work fast. From the water, from the cradle, from the pier, they managed to move her hull gently back into the V of the cradle and hammer in the wedges. She had almost been free, back in the water, like a runaway horse, but they managed to corral her. After what seemed like a long time, the cradle lurched forward on the tracks and *Marie*, tethered, was pulled up out of the water and led back into her stable.

"She seems sad," Anne said to Jeanine as they tossed the lines back on the stern.

Jeanine looked at Anne. "Yes, she is sad. She belongs in the water, as a wild animal belongs in the forest. But she is not yet ready. She would perish. No?"

"Right," Anne said. Tears pricked behind her eyes. She didn't know why.

The boathouse went quiet again. Jeanine pulled Anne's arm. "We have to go."

Pierre appeared at the side-door stairs, Alain beside him. Louis and Eric crowded in behind him. Pierre started up again, yelling in rapid French. He was directing his anger to Anne. He took to the stairs. Jeanine lurched backwards, yanking Anne with her. "We run now!" They ran down the dock and scurried out to the car. The low sun tinted the dust orange as Anne was once again sped in retreat over the back roads of the delta.

Back at the Slaters' house, Rod told them what had happened, when he got back from the yard. Pierre had called Eric Trubert, one of the original troops on the beaches of Dunkirk. Trubert was a famous race-car driver after the war who started a successful trucking business. Trubert borrowed a lorry for Pierre, who was going to take the boat away and hide her where no one would ever find her. They were in the process of backing her out of the boathouse onto another slipway so she could be picked up by the travel lift and put on the trailer. And the boathouse would have been empty.

There was another screaming fight among the men. Rod had been left out of the caper. He was also left out of core decisions, such as Pierre's, to hide the boat. Rod thought it was because Anne was friends with them now. As for Alain, he wanted to steal *Marie* and keep her for himself.

It was apparent to Anne that it was crucial to save *Marie Celine*, before she was destroyed or disappeared.

Anne contacted her father. It was then that Colin R. Neville embarked on the second most extraordinary journey of his life.

FIFTEEN

The Battle Begins

I HAD TO see the boat. However, between Cici and Annie, I was practically hog-tied to my rooms when we reached the hotel in Valras. Dr. Van had given us strong pills for jet lag.

Resigned, I took one dissolved in a dram of brandy and slept for a day in the shuttered rooms of M. Riquet's hotel. As soon as I awoke, late afternoon, a bowl of café au lait with plates of warm baguettes and jams appeared on my bedside table. Then in a terrible rush, Annie trundled me and Cici into the cab of a borrowed truck and sped us straight away to Rod Slater's vineyard home. As we jolted along the dirt road, I exalted, "I've never felt more refreshed, ready for action. In fact, I've never felt younger and stronger in my life!" Ci raised a dubious brow to Annie, who grinned mischievously.

But Ci's doubting posture did not deter me. I was going to find my lovely *Marie Celine*. Rescue her. Lost reserves of testosterone had been miraculously discovered and were pumping through my veins as we pulled up to the home of the first dragon I had to slay: Slater.

The warm welcome from the Slaters took the wind out of my sails. Ci saw me visibly huffing as we went down the long hallway to the kitchen. "Love-love, you have to calm down. There's a cultural protocol. Don't be too direct, love." Annie sighed, "Da-aad!"

"Righty-oh."

Cici hoarsely whispered, "And don't use that old phrase, 'righty-oh' Colley! Please."

I was dutifully subdued.

When we were seated at the lovely old wooden table, I faced Rod Slater. I had heard his story and he had heard mine. It was as if we really had known each other a long, long time. I must say, he was a rough-looking chap. He had to be older than I, but it was difficult to tell. The bashed-in fighter's face and thick, hard arms had a tanned, stretched, pigskin-texture. I could not help but notice the bluish-red, knobby stump that used to be his left hand and wrist. I noticed the right fist resting on the table was not clenched, but nearly so. His eyes looked anxious and a bit sad, I think. Thank God, however, this man came right to the point.

He smiled self-consciously. "I feel like I know you, Colin." I nodded and opened my mouth to say something, but Rod intervened. "I know you're wanting to see *Marie*. It's a bit of a tricky business on my end, you see." He cleared his throat. "Actually, we can't see the boat for a couple of hours. I've got keys. But we've got to be sure the yard's empty and that our chaps are gone. Tonight there's a parish meeting at the St. Nazaire church. That's in Beziers. They'll be going to the bistro after – a ritual for them. Pierre, Eric and Louis. Sometimes I go. But I'm not a Roman, you know."

"I see..." I said, staring at little dark dents and cuts in the worn table.

He took a deep breath and pulled a *pichet* to the center of the table between us. "We've prepared some food. It won't be long now." He set out wine glasses and wiped them with a napkin. "So, you believe this mystery boat, *Marie,* is your family boat."

I felt in my gut that aching longing. "From my talks with Anne, yes." I looked up at his open, blunt face and nodded solemnly. He poured our wine and held up his glass, toasting, "May we get this all straightened out, Colin. But I can tell you here and now, it's not going to be easy. This puts me in a damned awkward position, you know."

I nodded gravely. We sat in an odd silence and sipped the soothing wine, each of us lost in our own thoughts. Suddenly, with a forced cheeriness he said, "Like this wine?"

I regarded the wine for the first time, the light rose colour and the strawberry nose. "It's our Grenache." He said this with pride, took a deep breath and fell silent again, brooding.

"It's very good." I did mean it. I wished I could have enjoyed it. I shifted on the bench. "Now look here, Rod, I can't wait any longer. I feel as though I am going to spring right out of this seat! We are wasting time here."

"We have to wait. Can't risk getting hurt. Pierre is fiercely protective of *Marie.*"

I knew I had to be calm. Rod appeared to have become an ally. I had to calm down.

The women had gathered by the cooking area at the rear of the kitchen, preparing food and murmuring low. Cici's French was bubbling up from her childhood school lessons. Her attire her usual rich bohemian style—fit the French sense of fashion: a skirt of the brightly coloured fabric of Provence, white blousy T-shirt, batik scarf, and espadrilles. Annie, of course, had not changed out of her designer fatigues. And thankfully, Jeanine's English was quite good enough to bridge the language gap and save the day. The women got on fine; it seemed they'd known each other for generations.

Finally, Rod asked, "You came away with nothing from your family? No memory until recently? Did your sister have old photos or something of that sort?"

I felt the coolness of the wine throughout my body. I was resigned to this last couple of hours before I could see my *Marie.* "Cici is a half-sister. She never met our father. Born and raised in Nova Scotia. Her mother had a few old photos of our dad when he was very young, but they didn't help me. Nothing restored my memory. No…"

Rod digested all this a moment, then, "You never went back to England? Never wanted to?"

"All my family had been lost in two wars. Cici is my only family, you see. Actually, I could not recall anything. I simply had this gap, this dark space in my life that I longed to know. You Rod? Never returned?"

"No mate, didn't give it a thought. I lost all family. And I lost my hand. Back in England, I had just passed into an apprenticeship as a journeyman boat builder in 1939— a family profession for genera-tions…when the war happened." He sighed wistfully. "However, I never would've met Jeanine. She made up for all of it. Love of my life."

"Love of my life," I repeated, thinking of the one in my dreams. Lizbeth. I reached for my briefcase. "I've brought some photos of my work. I, too, must have had a vocation in boat building or woodworking. You see, I was driven to make models, line drawings, half-models. So many of them represented *Marie*. Or at least, what I felt she looked like. None of this was a conscious thing. It was a rather primal memory. I'd no records to go on." I passed the papers across to Rod.

He held them up, held them down, put them on the table, stood over them, turned them at different angles. I waited, listening to the hum of women in the background. Out the Slater's kitchen windows, a wind leaned against chestnut trees. Cypress tops, black-green against a pinkish sky, bowed and dipped. Poppies in the fields made little fans of varied reds and oranges as the wind swept them here and there. Rod studied on. What was taking him so long? At length, Rod set the papers aside. "Remarkable, to do these models and drawings without the subject at hand. Excellent." Then, with a wry smile he said, "You know, I slept in the forward stateroom."

"Annie told me."

"Can you tell me what I found hidden in a compartment under the bunk?"

I glanced shyly around, reddening. "Yes, there were some letters from my sweetheart, Elizabeth Whitehead. And I believe some love-sick replies I had written to her. Never mailed. I had some bullet casings I'd found on the Dover cliffs, a few of my favorite pink-grey marbles, the Spanish dagger that was forbidden by my mother. Odd, all those little things mean a great deal to me, just as they did when I was fourteen." Rod waited. The kitchen chatter quieted. I felt I turned a deeper shade of red. "Hard to recall all of it. Some odds and ends that boys keep." Rod waited. "Oh, and yes," I said quite softly, "a packet of playing cards, rather dicey, and a stack of French postcards. Rather racy."

"Rather!" laughed Rod. "They gave me such entertainment during my voyage."

"Dad!" Annie blurted. "That's disgusting. You didn't tell me that! What if I had found those things?"

"Well, my dear, 'things' are much more graphic these days, as I am sure you young people know."

A relieved laughter rang out about the room and we ate.

We ate boiled artichokes with butter and lemon juice, deep-red tomatoes from Jeanine's garden, topping a salad Niçoise washed down with bottles of red from Cote Rotie. Pleasant bits of conversation drifted around like aromas from the food. The wine relaxed me a bit. However, I still felt undercurrents of the anxiety of waiting for a battle. Listening to the chatter made it worse. I wished they would all shut up this polite chitchat.

Abruptly, Rod broke in."If this is your family boat. What do you plan to do?"

"My desire, my dream in my life? I want to take her to England. I learned recently that the Association of Little Ships is going to have a reenactment of the evacuation of Dunkirk. Yes. After finding *Marie Celine* and saving her, I want to sail her in the reenactment of the voyage of the Little Ships in May 2000. From Dover to Dunkirk!"

I heard flatware drop. I heard Rod make a raspy, hawking sound. He let out a cough and drank some wine. I heard Annie suck in her breath and whisper, mortified, "Dad! There's no time!" Cici stared at me in mute astonishment.

Rod set his glass down with a clunk and said slowly, "I see. Oh shit. There's going to be a row. A hell-of-a-row. I'm warning you." Then to himself, "Christ, if you do try to claim her, they'll never let you move her to England!"

* * * *

There was no moon. A slight breeze moved the treetops, black against the dusky cobalt sky. Rod and I drove the river road to the boat-yard in the flatbed. The women followed in Jeanine's car. Rod opened the side gates and we parked near the boathouse. We attempted to tread lightly over the uneven cobblestones. Occasionally someone would scuff or stumble. A curse and a shush. Rod's torch was not adequate to light the way for the five of us. Single file, we snaked up the stone steps and came out on the mezzanine inside the boathouse.

I could see we were on a platform over the shape of a boat. I heard a sigh. The wind called my name. "Colley," it said. "Colley-boy." A tremble rolled through me.

From behind, Annie held onto my waist with both hands and squeezed. "What is it, Dad? You're shaking."

I murmured something. I don't remember what. Annie gently pushed me up behind Rod as he waited to help us down the stairs leading to the main room. In the dusk, as soon as I saw her shape, I lost my breath. Anne tucked her arm under mine and supported me.

Rod lit two hurricane lanterns on a workbench.

"Better we use lanterns," he said. "The shop lights are for boat working. Very strong, like a bloody football stadium. Ah, we'll be right with these. No worries." One lantern was left low on the workbench, and Rod moved ahead, carrying the other.

The lantern lifted a veil of darkness from the copper-sheathed keel, up to the paint-peeled, oak-planked sides and up, illuminating her bow's knife-sharp edges in the shadows. I cried out, "It's her! My *Marie Celine*. By God! Oh God." Everyone paused, as if in reverence for the holy. I stood in awe of her almost ethereal presence.

Rod snapped to. "Right. We've not got much time. Are you ready Colin?"

"Yes. I'm quite ready." I was quivering with excitement.

Rod led the way up the ladder and down the hatch. He immediately lighted a kerosene lantern in the galley to the left, for me to see my way down. When I stepped down the companionway stairs, sailor style, with both hands on the rails, I could have done it with my eyes closed. It all came back. I was a kid again. I knew those stairs so well. So well.

When I hit the floorboards at the bottom and looked around in the lantern light I was stricken with emotion. I moved forward and off to the starboard alcove where my father's chart table stood. I ran my fingers over our old books. I lifted the tabletop; my father's parallels lay in the same place, the brass hinges now green with age, green as the brass dividers, in their place, next to the parallels. Even the pencils were there; they had the teeth marks exactly where he used to chew them; his old whittling knife with the horn handle, he used for sharpening his pencils—all still there. The knife was out of place. I moved it back into its tiny groove, next to the pencils. Tears fell freely on the instruments.

The others came down and stood back in the galley by the iron coal stove. I slid out from the chart table and moved to the main saloon. I ran my hands over the main dining table and sat on my mother's cushions. The table had been stained by coffee cups and glasses. The varnish was checked and split. I rubbed at the stains with my sleeve, tried to get them out. Mum's upholstery was threadbare; little tufts of velvet stuck out like stray hairs on a bald man's head. *Well, that can be made up to scratch in no time*, I decided.

I moved across to the starboard settee by the parlour stove and opened the stove door. Ashes had not been cleaned out. We lived aboard that last cold winter in the boatyard, before the war. We sat around that fireplace nightly, listening to BBC…to Hitler's speeches. Mum knitted, or sewed. I tied flies, did homework. Dad sketched designs for the boat and sipped his ever-present Scotch, while the winter storms of England passed over us. I gazed down on us gathered by the stove. How lovely. Lovely. Tears were salty, running into the corners of my mouth.

I went into my parents' stateroom. The mattress had been removed. Mahogany shelves, raised paneling, bookcases and tables were still covered with layers of varnish, now dull, lacking years and years of freshening up. It smelled damp. I opened one of Mum's drawers. There were a rosary and a small King James Bible. The bible was blue with mould. A few bone hairpins were in the back corner; I put them in my pocket. I sniffed and sniffed and could not find her lavender scent. Why on earth did I think I could? But then suddenly, she was there. I could smell her in the air, past the dank odors. "Mum?" I thought.

"Is that you Mum?" I turned round and round, expecting to see her.

On the bulkhead was our little gallery of photos. The frames, boat-style, had been screwed to the bulkhead. There were Mum and Dad, as I knew them. Tanned, windblown, hardy, smiling and happy. There was Dad, hammering the caulking irons that pushed oakum into the hull between the planks. He had turned with a silly smile, pipe clenched in the side of his mouth, bushy brows raised, hanks of thick white hair in his face, and click. Mum and Dad on the beach, and me between them – they each held one of my hands. We were all sandy and wet. God, I was a gangling, rangy-looking kid. Oh, there was Mum on a good day at the helm of *Marie*. Her bobbed hair is frozen back by wind. She is laughing, looking up at the sails. I was there. You can see my skinny leg on the bottom corner of the photo. I fell to my knees and had a good quiet cry.

After, I didn't know how long, the door opened. Rod stuck his head in. "You right, mate? You've gone missing in here a while."

"Oh, yes. Quite right." I dried my eyes with my sleeve.

He sniffed and scanned the cabin. "You know, Pierre never used this stateroom. His wife used to air out the linens and drawers. Like she was housekeeping for your parents. That's been a long time now. After Pierre's wife died, it's stayed much like this. Still smells fresh, like lavender, don't it? Your mum and dad's stuff is packed away here, in the yard, somewhere. Maybe at the Jeantot's house. Pierre used to believe that he would return the *Marie* to the owners. That was ages ago. I think over the years, he became too attached, couldn't let go of her, you see. He spends his days with her, down here at the table among his journals and logs and a bottle of wine. Now, he hangs on, as if *Marie* gives him a sense of who he is, a sense of his life and young man's courage. You know, we all need that."

"Yes, I think I do know."

Rod looked around, anxious, apologetic. "We've got to hurry, mate. We've been here too long already."

We moved up past the step where the main mast should be, to a bulkhead. As we moved up forward, Cici, Jeanine, and Anne were following, listening, running their fingers over woodwork, carved moulding and leaded glass panes, whispering reverently.

We made our way up to the forward stateroom. I found myself immersed in childhood wonder as I lifted the mouldy mattress and opened the little trap door in my bunk. "My God! It's all still there." Rod helped me get the packets out of the hiding place.

"I'll be damned." He grinned.

Everything was still there. And more. Things I'd forgotten. My jigs, favourite flies. Feathers from what bird? I can't recall. I found my pocketknife. The one Dad gave me, like his own, with a bone handle. It was seized shut with rust. Here were packets of mouldy love letters, and the dirty playing cards and postcards. "Oh my!" I picked the brass nameplate from the bottom of the box. At that moment, an explosion went off, and a blast of light beamed in through the scuppers. Old instincts caused us to hit the floorboards and cover our heads. The girls screeched. We yelled to them to take cover. I shoved the nameplate down the back of my Levies. Rod saw; he said nothing. We buried the box in its hole. Another blast went off.

"What the hell is that?" I whispered. "Shotgun?"

Rod hit his forehead with the palm of his hand. "Pierre. Shit. Shit. Shit." He hit his head several times, "Stupid. Stupid. Stupid me!"

We ran crashing into each other to get aft. What appeared to be a searchlight beamed down the main hatch. The women hurried off into the galley, out of the way.

"What is this?" Jeanine insisted.

"Stay down. It's Pierre. Drunk. With his ancient hunting gun." Rod moaned.

"Come out you English! Impostors. Trespassers. Thieves!" we heard him yell in English. His voice was deep, almost guttural. More like a growl. I tried to match the man with the voice. Big?

I assessed the women. Cici looked perturbed, impatient, in her unruffled, *grande dame* way. Jeanine looked stern, prepared for battle. And Anne, well she looked shocked; her jaws were working; her nostrils flared.

"Wait here." Rod climbed up the companionway and stood on the top step, shading his eyes against the harsh light. "Damn it all, Pierre, turn down those bloody shop lights."

"Slater? You? I should have known! You English!"

"Pierre…you know in your heart Colin Neville is not an impostor. He's the true…" and he ran off into rapid French that I could not decipher. More voices sounded in what was a frightful uproar.

Another shot went off. We all jumped. I climbed up the stairs behind Rod and managed to fit my head out the hatch next to him. Below were three men. Pierre, the one waving the gun, was wearing suspenders, an old-fashioned dress shirt and baggy trousers. He was short, bowlegged, white-haired and bearded. Fierce-looking, I must say. Next to him was a dapper-looking older man, taller, with slicked yellow-grey hair. He had the look of casual elegance, as one out on a sports car rally. That had to be Eric Trubert. Louis, I recognized straight away from Annie's descriptions: the halo of woolly hair, the bent, thin frame, sweet face, and the white skin of one who worked a lifetime indoors.

"Pierre! Put down that gun!" Rod yelled half angry, half frightened.

Pierre growled, "I am not going to shoot a person. I desire to make noise!"

"That you have done, my friend," Rod placated. "That you have done. Now put it down."

"They have come to take our *Marie*. It is known even in Beziers… Beziers!" With defiant flare and flash, he shoved the gun on to a workbench.

Louis, in a childish manner, spoke softly, "I do not want the gun to shoot. I do not want to shoot." And he warily set the gun back, out of reach, pointed it to the wall and set the safety. Pierre snatched a newspaper from Eric's hand. "This! This evening's paper!" He waved the newspaper. "We see this in Beziers. Evening paper!"

"Hold on…" Rod yelled down to Pierre. Then to me, hushed, "It's clear. Let's go." We climbed out of the boat and down the stairs, to come face-to-face with Pierre, who stood out in front of his group. He held the paper out to Rod while scowling at me up and down, from my tattered boat moccasins, to my scuffed Levis, my denim shirt, and the tip of my white head.

Anne was right; Pierre looked fierce, like an old, sore bear. I began, "Now see here…"

Pierre yelled, "Silence!" Eric and Louis stood stiff and battle-ready behind Pierre. A hoary, ragtag troop.

Rod held up his hand, infantry fashion. He read the article with growing amazement. I bent over his shoulder, looking at the French newsprint. He muttered, "Oh, shit. It's in all the English papers. The article was picked up by the French press. Released on the streets this evening. How in the hell…Colin? It says here that you're taking *Marie* back to England. That you're going in the 2000 sailing of the Little Ships. Mate, I believed you. I believed you just thought that up, you know? Just now. You confided in me. Even your sister, your daughter, were shocked at your announcement. How'd the media get hold of this information?" Rod looked dismayed, pained. Pierre's group looked menacing.

"Rod, I haven't one idea as to how, who…" Something hit me. I had learned of the 2000 reenactment of the Little Ships from…

Graydon's voice rang out, "Man. I'm sorry. I let you down. One of the *Times'* reporters ran with it. I didn't know, Colin. Honestly." Graydon appeared in the spotlights.

"Graydon?" I stammered. "How on earth?"

"This guy said you'd be here. Showed me the way." Another figure hurried behind him into the light. He was a good-looking young man, though projecting an intensity that was quite on fire. Pierre's troop was huffing impatiently. The women came down.

"Alain!" Anne whispered in my ear. "That's him! The ratty grandson who wants our boat!" She was up behind me; Cici and Jeanine hooked arms beside her. The women formed their own line of defense. "Graydon?" Anne called out loud. "Don't get near that creepy Alain. He's going to steal the boat!" Violent arguments, in French, broke out among Pierre's faction and Alain.

Graydon appeared harried. His usual slicked-back hair and tidy, edgy black clothes were rumpled; his posture was bent, as if he'd run a marathon in his business suit. He shaded his eyes and looked out toward us. "What? Anne? That you? I can't hear over all this noise."

Anne moved a few steps forward, pointing her finger at Alain, "That guy's going to ruin everything. He's going to steal the boat."

As she said this, Pierre and Eric shuffled forward. Louis inched up behind them. I could match that Pierre. I balled my fist. Graydon leapt through to my side. We hunched our shoulders and stood in what I guessed was a fighter's stance. A commotion at the back distracted us. The police arrived.

"These people broke into my shop and boatyard. Arrest them!" Pierre's voice cracked with anger.

Cici, Anne, Jeanine, Rod and I were all taken into custody. They arrested poor Graydon as well. He whined, "I'm losing my job over this. Sure as shit. Shit, damn it to hell…"

SIXTEEN

Battle Ready

*W*E WERE HELD, they said, for a cooling-off period, and released around midnight. All of us, save the Slaters, went to M. Riquet's hotel to sleep. Rod and Jeanine, local heroes arrested? Ruffled and highly insulted, they went home, promising to return with new plans. Graydon wandered off to his room, mobile phone pasted to his ear.

Later in the morning, when I went to wake Anne, she was gone. She came back to us later, as we assembled in the hotel dining room for a strategic breakfast. Her fatigues doubly wrinkled and unattractive, her uncombed hair erupting with cowlicks, she plunked down by Cici and put her feet on the chair in front of her. She leaned over and filled us in on her activities.

Anne had risen early on a mission. She walked across the alley to the back door of Chez Louis, where Louis and Alain were preparing food for the day. She found Alain alone, washing dishes. She accused Alain of calling the police. He fervently denied this, explaining that calling the police was something his grandfather might've done. Disregarding him, she went on to charge his Grandfather Pierre for the crime of stealing *Marie Celine*. She cited his grandfather for hiding the boat all these years. And Alain, she said, was guilty of perpetuating this offence.

She told him the boat was on a list of unfound ships, put out by the British government. Alain informed Anne that his grandfather did not bother with modern inventions such as internet, computers, TV. And besides, he asked, why would his grandfather read some old English list? And he insisted that the boat was not stolen.

As Anne told us her story, her face reddened with mortification. Alain had asked her in return, why I, Colin Neville, waited sixty years to claim the boat. With this Anne told him about my war injuries and how I could not remember anything until recently. She said he sniffed disrespectfully. Then he announced that our game was up. He said his grandfather had hired a top maritime lawyer. This top lawyer was due in Valras any moment this very day. He said that his grandfather would win. At that juncture, Anne became very angry and was really going to tell him off. But he called her "an angry kitten" and left the room. She explained that the awful clatter we had heard earlier from the alley was her accidental bump into a table of cooking pans as she exited.

Anne finished her story with, "If I didn't hear that news about the lawyer, I'd have won that fight."

Cici and I let out a breath.

Anne crossed her arms. Her face was flushed with anger and her expression, unsure, pensive; it ran deep, like a passion, like a lava fissure in the earth of her soul. That's my girl. She's always been my little fighter.

My vexations were interrupted by a noise-storm from the outside entrance to the dining room. M. Riquet hustled into the room, looking side to side, as if being pursued by devils. "Hurry! *De violence!* A riot!"

Cici and I rushed for the door. Anne joined us. At the doorway, M. Riquet was ushering us out chanting, "A riot! Riot!" Graydon loped down the stairs, skipping steps, stuffing papers in his briefcase, and met us at the door. We four went out to the lane. M. Riquet hovered a distance behind.

There, across the way, lined up along the Petanque court, under the plane trees, was a phalanx of muttering, grumbling village seniors.

Heading the body of battle-ready old duffs were Pierre, Eric and Louis. My backers and I lined up on the curb on our side of the street. At that moment, Graydon left me. "Be just a minute…" he said, and hurried off, mobile phone to ear.

My remaining warriors were Ci and Anne. Riquet was hopeless.

Pierre Jeantot nudged forward a prissy-looking man dressed in a baggy grey suit, clutching a briefcase under his arm. "Monsieur Carnet, maritime lawyer," Jeantot shouted triumphantly. "The boat is ours. Law says: salvage rights. We are legal!" The lawyer nodded emphatically.

I was shot through by conflicting emotions: abject fear of losing my *Marie* again and piercing anguish, and fury. The fury won out. "Now see here, Jeantot! You may be quite right. But over my dead body will you get my *Marie Celine*! This boat is mine. You must understand. I was raised in that boat. She was the only home I knew. This is like stealing someone's ancestral home, someone's land, someone's family, someone's dreams. We all know it has all been done before in history. This does not make it right!" A murmur of affirmation from my two girls.

Pierre's arms flung up into the air. "I did not steal anything. *Marie* came to me! To us!" Grunts and growls of approval from Pierre's group.

"Yes, the boat found us. She saved us," Eric put in.

From the back of the crowd someone yelled, "After you, the English, left us, the French, to die by the hands of the enemy! Left us to die on the beaches of Dunkirk. That's what you did!"

Cold outrage ran through me. My voice carried strong above the din: "Mum and Dad were killed coming back for you…the French! Mum said, 'We must go back for our French boys.' And we did. The Channel weather was clearing. Stukas were swarming like locusts, bombing the last of the English ships. Mum and Dad died that day! I was shot up…an invalid for years. We came back for you that day. You, French! We were willing to give our lives for you. How dare you! How bloody dare you!"

Outrage, fueled by adrenaline, thrust me toward Pierre. Pierre's group took steps forward.

Rod and Jeanine turned up at my side with Ci and Anne and held me back. Suddenly, Pierre's troop backed down.

A commotion from up the street turned all heads.

"Hold on! Everybody just hold on!" Graydon called out. Graydon lead an irregular column of three worn-out travellers dragging travelling bags. The first, behind Graydon, was a tall, stately woman in a white suit. Her hair was gunmetal-grey and tied up in a loose bun. She was stout and broad in the hips, which gave her walk a rolling motion. Behind her was a bald-headed, ruddy-faced, beefy chap. He had a rigid, military bearing, and a neat military mustache. He wore a navy-blue blazer, white shirt, navy-gold striped tie and white slacks, and walked with a pronounced limp. Following him was a tall, gaunt gentleman. He sported a short-cropped white beard and white hair. A tweedy jacket, vest, starched cotton dress shirt and Oxford tie gave him that buttoned-down, academic appearance. I gazed on these spectral images coming towards me in the noon's white light. As they came closer, I focused. Some things one remembers—the carriage of the head, the manner of a gait, the straightness of back, the stance.

My God, I had known these people! They were young with me once. They had stayed with me, over the years, appearing in the prisms of light that flicked through my brain. An uneasy feeling washed over me. I feared I was no longer lucid.

"Who are those people with Graydon?" Anne asked.

"If I am not mistaken, they are my dreams come to life," I said. At once these were no longer elderly strangers. They were young, vibrant people.

Anne clutched my arm protectively. " Dad, you're not going wonky on me again, are you?"

Cici peered into the glare.

The large woman, quickening her step, rolled up to me, dropped her bags and enveloped me in an embrace. An embrace like I had never had before. I felt the exuberant buttresses of her rounded body pressing against me.

"Colley! Oh, Colley, you look ever-so-lovely!" Her voice had not changed. Still a melodious soprano with joyous trills. I used to think it awfully girlish, silly. Now it sounded like music of the spheres. I was speechless.

She pulled back and gave me a good look. Her cheeks had that out-of-doors healthy, apple-skin tint; her cupid's bow mouth still red, wet, and perfect. No make-up. She did not need it. Wind and sun wrinkles etched her tight-skinned face. Grey-blue eyes matched that grey hair all tied up in loose waves and knobs. Odd. None of that English reserve here. Just like when we were kids, she was uninhibited, bold, bubbling over with jollity.

Finally, after clearing my throat, I exclaimed, "Elizabeth Whitehead. Lizbeth!"

Also before me were Mad Mal Mackay and Rutherford. I was staggered. "Why you've not changed a bit!" My eyes saw them as they had been, young men on the beaches of Dunkirk.

"Colley!" Rutherford half laughed, half cried.

"Colley lad," Mal blustered, controlling his emotions with a visible effort, holding his breath, pushing out his chest, mouth turned down.

At last we let go our emotions and fell into a hug.

Pierre's group stood back, shaking their heads and mumbling.

Our reunion was interrupted by a clamour down the street. A tangle of press people, cameras, cables, was uncoiling towards us. Oh my.

"*Merde*," I heard Pierre say. "*Merde, merde, merde,* " echoed through the French faction.

"What the hell?" Graydon faltered. "It's the press. Hoards of them. We can't let them catch us here." He looked frantically around for a hiding place.

"Let's get the hell out of here!" Rod hollered, gathering us in a close bunch and herding us toward Louis's cafe. Pierre's gang cut us off when they reached the door first. They crowded in and slammed shut the heavy door, locking us out. For a second we were trapped, the media bearing down on us. Then the door opened and Louis hauled us in, locking the door behind us.

SEVENTEEN

The War Effort

*B*ANDED AT THE door, our eyes adjusting to the sudden change from blazing southern sunlight to the cool, dark interior of Louis's bistro, we assessed our situation. Through the far windows we could see the village support team along with press people lingering outside the patio. Pierre, Eric and the lawyer, M. Carnet were at the bar, peering over their wine glasses at us. We returned their look. No one spoke.

Louis, in chef's apron, watched from the kitchen; perspiration glowed on his forehead.

He came from behind the bar and in his sweet, compelling manner urged Pierre's group to a trestle table, where they milled about the benches, making grumbling noises. He ushered us to the opposite side of the table.

Louis eased food and wine down the center of the table. Hands in pockets, shrugging shoulders, shuffling feet, our groups did a slow dance on our opposite sides of the table. Finally, after a long, tense silence, I motioned our side to sit down. My companions and I scooted along our bench, glaring down the opposition as they lined the other side. Jeanine, Elizabeth, Anne, and Graydon stood behind, by the bar. Alain was behind the bar looking on with a dark expression. Pierre's group stared us down. We stared back, daring.

Then broke out a tumult of false accusations, overblown, bold statements, profuse emotions, threats.

"*Marie* is part of our village," Eric said.

"A symbol of our freedom," Louis spoke softly.

"Why then, was she held captive in a boat shed all these years? Out of sight. Decommissioned," I demanded.

"She was not hidden. She was simply put away until we could care for her," Pierre defended.

"We were going to make a monument for her. In the village. A hero's monument. A hero for the Resistance," Eric affirmed.

"But yes," Louis said to the group, "we were going to restore her. All of us."

Rod offered, "Time. We just needed more time."

"Bullshit!" Mal said. "That boat hasn't been touched in years! We'll buy the bloody boat! No limits on price! We'll get a fund. An association to save her. Have professionals restore her."

"One cannot sell a spirit!" Pierre raged. He beat the table with his fist. "*Marie* is not leaving us!"

"One cannot steal and hold a spirit," I spat out. Graydon looked on, greatly disturbed.

"We've retained a barrister in London…" Mal started.

The lawyer announced, "You will lose. The Right to Salvage Law is international."

"None of this will do. *Marie Celine* has to sail with the Little Ships! There's no time for this!" I cried.

"Our Angel Ship is staying here!" Pierre stood up and banged both fists on the table.

Dishes clattered. Wine glasses tipped, bouncing and clanking on the table.

I rose. "She's not your boat. She's my boat!" I banged the table harder, making ear-shattering clatters.

"You have no proof, Neville." Pierre nodded to the others, who grumbled in noisy agreement.

I pulled the bronze nameplate from my hip pocket and displayed it inches from Pierre's face. His eyes widened with recognition, then fear, then anger. "How...? How did you get that?"

My head was menacingly close to Pierre's. My eyes stung. I was sure, if I lit a match, he would have ignited into a puff of flames off the Pernod on his breath. He clutched my shoulder, giving me a start, and tried to grab the nameplate, but missed. It clattered to the floor. He shoved me backwards. I recovered and gave him a shove.

Pierre ran his hand over his face and glared, disbelieving. "You English!" He shoved me again. I shoved him back. He fell back, stumbled, and climbed over the table after me.

Mal stepped in blocking him. "That's it for you, Frenchy!"

Eric moved around the table, grabbed Mal, and pulled back, knocking Mal off balance.

Rutherford stepped up, "Bastards!" And pushed Eric with all his weight. Pierre and I were jostled this way and that, as though tumbling in a wave.

Rod jumped in trying to separate us. Louis edged up to the pack, "We cannot do this! No more! Stop!"

Rutherford was knocked back and fell into Louis, sending his bony frame across the room, into the girls, "Oh, pardon..." He tried to move, and in a blur, I thought I saw Lizbeth hold him back.

Alain rushed forward. "Stop this!" He was trying to break it up when there was a muted crump. All of us veterans of Dunkirk froze. There followed a smaller explosion. At that moment, villagers hammered on the locked back door, screaming in French.

"The boatyard's on fire," Alain yelled out, as he sprinted to unlock the heavy latch. "*Marie Celine!*" Pierre and I cried out at once. He and I dashed for the door. Dazed, the rest of the group hung back a second, then leapt forward.

There was a scramble. Crammed in the doorway first, Pierre and I saw black smoke smudging the azure sky. My heart thumped. I felt my breath ebb. My hands were wet. I couldn't lose her. Not again. It would kill me. Pierre looked at me, his eyes lifeless, still with dread. I knew he felt the same way.

Confusion erupted behind. Eric pushed through, "*Allez!*" Pierre, Eric, Alain, Rutherford, Mal, Rod, Louis, Anne, and I piled into Eric's lorry. Graydon, with cameras slung over his shoulders, jumped on the tailgate and rode with us. Eric sped to the boatyard, swerving to miss villagers running to the fire.

In the truck bed, I was squished next to Rod. He yelled above the din, "It's down by the old fuel dock and paint shacks. Hell! Old fuel tanks, kerosene, oil, bins of rags. Damn it to hell! Pierre! He should have cleaned this place up years ago."

"How close is the fire to *Marie Celine*?" I could barely get the breath to speak. It came out as a whisper. He said, "What?" I repeated close to his ear.

"Fire's still down at the bottom of the yard, by the receiving dock. The big basin. Boathouse is up the river in the smaller basin. Not there yet." I had only been to the boathouse; I had not seen the rest of the yard; at that time it was dark.

When we pulled up to the main gate, villagers had already got bucket brigades going. Alain and Anne leapt out and ran to help. Pierre lumbered after them, bellowing in French. I heard approaching sirens. There was a jumble of people and a cacophony of shouts and screams.

Pierre motioned to me to follow. The fire department arrived. I ran after Pierre through clusters of work sheds to *Marie Celine's* boathouse.

Rod came up and we followed as Pierre ran to the side of the boathouse.

"*Marie Celine!*" I yelled, seeing smoke and sparks carried towards us on the freshened wind. We came to a shack by the boathouse. I helped uncover a machine from under years of storage. We lugged it into the daylight.

"Pump!" Pierre panted with excitement. I had seen such a suction pump before; it had two handles, one on each side of a barrel, seesaw fashion. Rod found couplings and hooked up a snake's nest of hoses.

The main hose ran into the river. Pierre and I each grabbed a handle, Rod aimed the hose and we pumped river water over the boathouse and surrounding buildings. Years of neglect had sprouted thick, tufted growths of sun -dried foliage on the broken roof tiles.

Switching off jobs, we pumped, and we pumped, and we pumped to save *Marie Celine.*

By late afternoon, the fire was out. The chief reported to Pierre, and Rod translated for me. The chief said it could have been the oil-soaked rags he found that started the fire. The fumes in the empty gas tanks could have been a factor. There had been a top ajar on one of the old underground tanks. Even a tossed cigarette from one of the seniors who fish off that dock could have been a cause. They were not sure.

Pierre blundered, "But we have no oil rags. We have not used that gas dock for years!"

The chief said that there would be an investigation. We were all fortunate it was not a big fire, he told us. He left a small crew of firemen behind wetting the ashes. The gas dock was gone, and the paint shed was destroyed, along with the rigging and sail loft. Rod said that the sail loft had not been used for years. The same with the rigging shop.

And the paint shed was filled with old, lead-based paint, illegal now, Rod said. All in all, there was not a great loss. It was decided that Rod would find the others.

With a dim spark of remaining adrenalin, Pierre and I hurried to the saved boathouse and approached *Marie Celine.* In my own thoughts, I stroked and petted her peeling bow. I laid my cheek against her. "Old Thing," I whispered, "my lovely, sweet Old Thing." Closing my eyes, I saw *Marie* as she had been, a proud schooner, lunging and leaping over the waves to save an army. I saw Pierre's feet on the other side of the bow. Was he doing the same thing? Making love to *Marie Celine?*

Our group dragged in. Pierre and I rounded the bow and waited. We did not make eye contact. Somberly, I observed Louis and Eric arm in arm; it was hard to tell who was supporting whom. Mal and Rutherford stumbled along, Mal favoring his bad leg, and Rutherford's usually erect, slim figure was slumped. Rod, Graydon, Alain, and Anne, dirty, dazed and weary, trailed in. The next moment, Jeanine and Lizbeth arrived, ushered by M. Riquet. They were subdued and brooding, for the firemen had not let them on the property. All gathered before Pierre and me, as if waiting for a profound revelation.

A silence fell. At the edge of this, I said, "What are we going to do now?"

"Angel Ship will not leave France!" Pierre wailed.

I turned to him, but said nothing. I felt a rip in my chest, a wrenching, painful division. I did not know what to do. Pierre loved *Marie* as much as I did. And I didn't want to share her, or my dream of saving her and sailing away. It was always *Marie Celine* and I. No one else. What would my *Marie* say about this? What would Mum and Dad say?

Silence fell once again. The group shuffled and rustled. They looked to Louis, who stepped forward.

"The Angel Ship is part of us all. And we are part of her. We go to the café. Rest. Break bread. If, that is, we are sure that a compromise can be made." Everyone nodded expectantly. I had a feeling that this matter had been discussed at length before they arrived here.

We were shuttled back to the café in M. Riquet's Eurovan and Eric's lorry. Silent and exhausted, we shambled back to our seats at the table. Lizbeth, Jeanine and Anne sat at the end of the table. Louis and Alain disappeared behind the bar. Graydon and Rod sat with the women.

Pierre lit a cigarette and looked at me sideways. "And so? How are we going to do this?" He raised his brows challenging.

I said, very carefully, "We both love this boat. She is part of us. All of us. She came into our lives when we needed her, and she carried us through. Imagine how distressed she must be with all this squabbling." I felt shot through with spiritedness and I seized upon it. "I say we share her! We can all care for her."

Pierre's jaw dropped, the cigarette dangling, "Then, our Angel Ship can stay here?"

"Yes," I said. "We will develop a sort of trust. We all chip in. After all, she has helped the war effort for France and England." The room was hushed.

"But," I said, "we must get her to the reenactment! It is most important. Yes!" I proposed, "She stays here in France most of the time. And when there is need for her to be in England for memorial events, then she will go, somehow. We will make it work. In the meantime she sails in her French holiday parades, memorial events here. And, I ask one more thing."

Pierre looked at me dubiously, "Yes?"

"I ask that we all go in the reenactment of the Little Ships. For we were all there."

Each side of the table was portentously quiet. Alain's expression opened into shock and then deep interest. Cici, Anne, Lizbeth, and Jeanine were holding hands under the table, their eyes closed, as if making a wish.

I waited.

Pierre stood, his face drawn with gravity. He put his hand across the table, "But of course. It is only right that we all sail Angel Ship with the Little Ships. I am agreed." We shook on it. Eric set the nameplate between us. Pierre slid it over to me. He let out a long sigh. "I will never forget that night when I put the plate in hiding from the Germans. It was a hell on earth. Hell on earth."

We stood a moment, each submerged in memories of the inferno of the Channel, the bombs thundering, Stukas diving, their guns flaming.

Lizbeth's melodic voice sang out, "This is a jolly good future for our *Marie Celine*!" She gave Anne, Jeanine, and Cici lavish hugs.

Rutherford sat up brightly. "I like this idea awfully!"

Mal regarded the group with a curious expression of half quizzical wince, half smile. "I think you've all gone off your heads, but count me in."

Grim, Alain looked on from the kitchen.

Joyous, Louis came forward with plates of food. He motioned to

Alain who, in a desultory manner, brought bottles of Cote de Rotie and glasses to the table. He set a glass by Anne; she turned up her nose. "Decaf?" she asked him.

"Ah, *non*." Alain replied arrogantly.

"Green tea?"

"Ah, *non*."

"Coffee?" She whined this time.

Alain rolled his eyes and sighed. "No. Wine only. That is all today. Wine."

Sourly, Anne accepted a glass and gave Alain the look of death. He shrugged and left.

We planned all manner of messing about with boat work. We huddled over our finances and budgets. An account would be set up in the local bank. It was announced that work would begin tomorrow. The press crews missed us as we exited through the back kitchen door.

EIGHTEEN

Geezers' Rebellion

*B*ACK AT THE hotel, M. Riquet had decided, "It is the English that I love. It is the Germans I do not like. They stay up all the night and sing German songs."

Well, since the baggage handlers had just gone on strike and the airports were shut down, and race riots had started up in Marseilles, we were lucky to have the whole hotel to ourselves. Mal, Rutherford, Lizbeth, Cici, and I settled in the library with cigars and port. Anne warned us from the landing, "You're all going to be major sorry when I give the wake-up call." She trudged upstairs to her room.

Graydon had dark circles under his eyes and a day's growth of charcoal stubble. He poured a brandy from the sideboard and wished us goodnight. "Graydon," I called after him. "Did you arrange this reunion?"

He looked over at us and thought a moment. "I and a cast of thousands. The miracle of *Marie Celine*."

We old friends remained in a past world that evening, blissful reminiscence in that smoke-filled room, listening to the music of old English cabarets, swing and jazz. I learned that my Lizbeth lost all family in the war, and the family farm had been bombed; the land was later sold. She took a job as an apprentice collecting primitive art for the museums. She spent her years in desolate outposts with indigenous peoples. "I found I enjoyed the textiles most of all. The weaving and the spinning, the materials, textures."

"Weaving? Spinning?" I felt heady.

"Oh, yes. Sheep's wool, llama, even flax."

"Brilliant!" I beamed. "Are you doing all that now?"

"Sadly, no. Last year, I broke my hip. Difficult climbing about mountain villages and arctic tundra, you know. So, here I am. Retired."

Mal stayed in the service and took a desk job in Singapore. He married a young Asian girl who moved her whole family in on him, and bit him for quite a lot of money. Poor chap returned to England, "To live out my life in peace."

Rutherford followed his dream and became a professor of fine arts at Oxford. He lived an academic life, but often he did pub crawls with Mal to shake off the remnants of the war.

We stayed up too late and drank a bit too much. We were not at all prepared for the rigours of the following day.

Graydon told me first thing in the morning that something was up. He told me the morning papers were sold-out on the streets of Valras and Beziers, Villaneauve and Agde. M. Riquet managed to secure a copy of the most popular newspaper for us. Surreptitiously, he slipped it to me at the breakfast table. I could see that *Marie* was in the news. Slater appeared beside me. "How's about I translate."

Slater read: "Do the people of France want to let a national treasure go to the English?" The newspaper declared how the French had very strong opinions on the role of the French Resistance, the Communists, the Royalists and the Gaullists (the party led by General de Gaulle, that won out in the end). Some said to bury the boat and what she symbolized. It seemed we had fomented an upwelling in French society, stirring a national dialogue on the war and politics that had, until now, been kept down in the deep. Astonishing as it appeared, we could cause some sort of rebellion. In France?

I passed the paper around the breakfast table. Graydon blanched, squinting painfully through his glasses. "Says here, the English are expecting *Marie Celine* back for the Little Ships' sailing. Shit. It also says that a newly formed group of old veterans and resistance fighters are not going to let her out of the country. It says that there are communist agitators stirring all of this crap up. Hell. It says the paper interviewed one of the agitators who said they were led by Paco Torres, one of the French army left on the beaches by the English." He hiked his glasses up on his nose and ran his fingers through already spiky, messy hair.

Lizbeth, Cici, Rutherford, Mal and Anne all spoke at once in variations on this theme. "We are here to help. As hard and as much as you need." Slater stood by me. "Count me in mate. And my Jeanine. If Paco is back in France, I will kill him. I'll hunt the cowardly traitor down."

When we entered the boathouse, Pierre, Louis, and Eric had the morning papers spread out on the table. Bowls of coffee, cigarette packets, ashtrays, tumblers of wine, and torn baguettes littered the ancient wood. Cigarettes dangling from their mouths, the Frenchmen looked up with a mixture of hostility and consternation. We wavered at the bottom of the stairs.

Pierre held up the paper and hit it with the back of his hand. "Did you see this?" he growled.

"Yes," I said.

"Do you understand this problem? This is a very big problem!"

"I believe so," I said cautiously, and prayed he would not quit our project.

He picked up the papers and flicked them with a snapping, violent pop. We all flinched. Pierre's deep, theatrical voice vibrated through the boathouse, "Well, I say we stand up for what is right. Our Free French Resistance…we stand up for *Marie*. If Paco Torres is behind this, he is a dead man. To hell with them!" With knobby hands, he crunched the papers into little balls and threw them on the floor.

"To hell with them," we echoed. "Let's get to work." The boatyard was once again up and running.

The women went below and pulled out the mouldy interior cushions, linens, and rusted, tattered household equipment.

Eric, Rod and Louis worked on the decks. Mal and Rutherford, Pierre and I climbed scaffolding and started scraping the hull to bare wood and reefing the hull seams. "It's me leg," Mal complained. Getting up the scaffolding was a problem for him, but once he got on the platform he was good to go. Rutherford was not an outdoors type, but he managed quite well.

When it was time to quit, we left our workstations and gathered round the table to fill our wine glasses. There was a general feeling of new strength, vitality. In proud silence we lifted our glasses to *Marie Celine*.

We arrived at the bistro starving and thirsty. The women were already there enjoying themselves. Grim and taciturn, Alain served us. M. Riquet joined in, lighting on the bench, next to my Cici. He kissed her hand. Anne snorted. Cici, Anne, Lizbeth, and Jeanine nattered away with a great deal more energy than we men could muster. I noticed that, quite definitely, Lizbeth's breasts jiggled when she laughed, as if they did their own little dance. I found it difficult to concentrate.

Anne shot withering looks of disapproval when Alain spilled red sauce over the table and on her sand- and camel-coloured desert-print fatigues.

Rod was late. He had lingered by his tool chest when we quit. Hungry, we hovered over our bowls of lamb stew like starving prisoners in a camp. Food was the meaning of existence at that moment. No sipping the tumblers of wine. Drank them down like water, we did.

Rod arrived at the side door and moved on tender knees and ankles up to the table, "Our *Marie's* got a broken stem!" Rod's jig-sawed face was blotched white and red. "A major structural problem. Could take months. It's special oak. How are we going to bloody find it? If we do bloody find it, how are we going to bloody fix it in time?" He folded onto the bench seat and slumped over the table, rubbing his head. The rest of us looked up startled, bewildered, wracked by the idea of impending defeat.

"Stem? How did this happen? Her stem was perfect!" Pierre slapped the table with his hands.

"I think it happened when she came down on the cradle beams the other day. Stem's cracked. Could have been rot in there. Don't know. Planks want to pull away from the stem. I saw it, just now. Scraped off the paint."

I remembered, "Yes, my dad used English white oak, I believe." Everyone looked at me expectantly. "Umm, sorry. Can't imagine where he found it. Somewhere in England."

Pierre slapped the table with each word. "We never order this wood any more. Not for years." He looked at us with a vacant stare, then shook his head, "Ah, it has been too long. I left these matters to the yard. I used to have men who did this kind of work. Who knew where to find any wood. They have all gone. Gone back to Barcelona." He looked up bewildered. "Unless Alain…?" He faded away in thought.

"Means, old cock, time you spoke to your grandchild," Rod hammered. "Best damn woodcraftsman in France."

Pierre looked like a man caught in a sin. It was God who caught him. Alain moved about the table, feigning detachment. Pierre looked up to heaven. Alain, insolent, rolled his clear black eyes, moved away, sighing dramatically and clattering dishes. Pierre finished his plea to the heavens and followed Alain into the kitchen.

NINETEEN

Sea Changes

M. RIQUET SHOOED us into the dining room in the early morning. Cici insisted on helping him. Her middle-school French was much improved. Around M. Riquet, her voice was musical and her manner coquettish.

"Aunt Ci's flirting, Dad."

I thought of all the years Cici had the responsibility of me. She never did have a beau.

Now that I was well, she seemed brighter. More carefree.

Anne whispered to me, wrinkling her nose, "Do people that old fall in love?"

Taking a deep breath, I had to think hard. "Do they? Well, hmm…" I was gratefully interrupted by Rod herding us out to work.

Another dazzling, white-light day opened upon us as we stepped through the ancient oak doors of the hotel. We were halted by a swarm of news media and protesters. Graydon rubbed his bloodshot eyes and peered at the crowd with weary disbelief. The protesters had hand-painted signs on old sheets and cardboard wine cases that said, "*Marie* belongs to the French!"

Lizbeth pulled me close. "Some protesters. They look more like a lynch-mob of octogenarians."

"I say!" I replied. She was right. The crotchety, scruffy seniors, some in workman's singlets and dirty trousers, some in suits that had seen too many Sundays, some in starched, round-collared dress shirts and woolen trousers held by braces, some in French army uniforms, many in wheelchairs, or on crutches. They gathered in a half-circle around us. Mal, Rutherford and I stepped up and barricaded the women. A beer bottle flew and smashed on the cobblestones. A wine bottle sailed and crashed not far from us. A tomato smacked on the dirt, splattering my shoes.

Graydon was livid. "I'm going to complain to the people in charge of this outrage! Unacceptable!" He was pummelled by a barrage of French curse words and rotten tomatoes as he marched off down the lane. Cameras captured all.

The mob closed in on us as we inched past their blockade. I stepped up my pace and led Anne, Lizbeth and Jeanine; we bluffed our way through and into Rod's lorry. As Rod drove away, the mob hobbled, wheeled, and stumbled after the erratic course of our escape vehicle.

Lizbeth looked back. "Good God, I didn't know the French rose so early in the morning."

We arrived in the boathouse to find Alain in baggy coveralls, on the scaffolding up by the bow. He worked alone with a sander, cleaning up the jagged hole where part of the stem had been cut out earlier. It lay on the workbench. Fascinated by this unexpected sight, we observed him in awe. His brown, lean body moved around the scaffolding with a catlike prowess I had never seen in this young man. A forelock of jet-black hair flopped over his eyes. Blowing away the coarse threads, he continued with an attitude of both resoluteness and bliss. Anne crossed her arms and looked up, watching him with pursed lips and wrinkled nose.

Cici whispered to Anne, "If you continue to make that face, it will freeze that way."

"Ci!" Anne hissed. She sucked in hard, let out a noisy, deep sigh. But she did relax her expression.

Rod broke the silence. "Hey mate, can we lend a hand?"

"Thank you, Rod my friend. It is done. Started at three this morning." Alain flashed a brilliant, proud smile. "The worst part is over!"

"Bravo!" blared Pierre's voice from the back of the building, where Pierre, Eric and Louis entered.

"I ordered the wood this morning." Alain was all business.

"Excellent!" Eric joined Pierre.

"Thank God he's back into his proper profession," bleated Louis, smiling with a touch of relief, and making a sign of the cross. "Dear God, may young Alain Jeantot never aspire to restaurant work ever, ever again. Amen." The others chuckled.

With his childlike sincerity, Louis widened his eyes, protesting, "God knows! This young man was born to be a craftsman. God also knows that I have mentored young Jeantot in the arts of the cuisine and he is hopeless! God will not be angry with me for wasting His time."

Jeanine motioned Ci, Elizabeth, and Anne to the side door. They reached the car just outside, and I saw Anne break off and come back into the boathouse. She announced to no one in particular, "They're a team on that sewing thing. I can't sew. And to be quite truthful, I've never liked that girlish stuff anyway. It was decided I could do more useful work here. So?" She blinked a few times and looked at us with anticipation.

"But of course!" Pierre rubbed his hands and looked about for input. We all chimed out our duties and offered to set her to work. From above, Alain called down. His resonant voice fell over us. "Mademoiselle could begin the mast work. No one has addressed the needs of the masts. Without them, *Marie* cannot sail. They must be varnished. Then, we are able to assemble the rigging on her."

Anne looked about in conjecture.

Alain swung off the scaffolding and landed beside her. "I will show you what to do. In the beginning it is quite rudimentary. I will work with you until the wood is delivered. By then, you may be on your own. If, of course, you are able to do this work."

Anne shrugged and crossed her arms.

Several cigarettes and coffees later, we resumed our hard labour. Anne slouched after Alain to the side of the boathouse where the masts were stored.

TWENTY

Bare Poles?

I HAD TO sharpen tools in the shop beside the boathouse. I oiled the whetstone and watched the kids moving the masts into place alongside my shed. Alain seemed a different lad these days. No more sulking and arrogant sniffs. No, Alain had an aura of contentment about him. His face was relaxed, even dimpled with a slip of a smile. He was bemused over his task, easy, confident, as if it were a sort of meditation for him. I watched while Alain gave Anne instructions.

She did have an obstinate bearing, hands on hips, nose in the air. I must say, she has always been on her own at home and used to being a bit bossy…a bit spoiled, actually.

They were standing by the mainmast. I couldn't help but chuckle when Alain handed her the Makita drill; he was very much the professor. "Now, Mademoiselle Neville, you must first put the driver in reverse to back the old screws out of the hardware." He showed her the speeds.

"Dad taught me all that stuff in his woodshop." And she fired up the driver and applied it to the first screw. There was a jackhammer noise as the driver glanced off the fastener and gouged the Sitka spruce wood of the mast. "Oh damn!" She looked mortified.

"Damn indeed, Mademoiselle." He pursed his lips thoughtfully. "Now, first allow me to finish my instructions this time. You must first loosen the brittle varnish filling the screw slots, with this." He took a hammer and hammered a slot screwdriver into the fastener's head, uncovering the groove hidden beneath years of dark gold varnish. He eased the drill from her fingers and handed her the tools. "Now you try, Mademoiselle."

Holding the tools, she stared at the damage she had done. "I can't believe I did that!"

Alain was studying her with a quizzical expression. "Mademoiselle?"

Anne screwed up her face. "Could you call me Anne? Pah-leeze?"

He laughed softly, "Ah, but of course, Anne." It sounded nice, the way he pronounced her name; it came out sounding like: *Ann-ah*. Very musical, this language.

I was relieved to see them settle into a diligent routine. Peace. After a time, Alain appeared against the sunlight in the door and peered into the cool shade of the shed. "Mr. Neville! I did not know you were here!" He smiled graciously. "I have to sharpen these drivers and chisels. Do you mind?"

"My dear lad, let me do it. You can carry on with something else."

He moved into the shop and placed the tool on the bench beside me. "Are you sure?"

"Quite. How are you doing out there? I hope my daughter is not abusing you."

He hesitated, thinking. "Your daughter is…special."

I laughed. "The English word would be spoiled. Anne is used to running the show. I must say, she rides herd on the goats, the sheep, our hired help, and local boys. Cici and I have been overindulgent and loving every moment." I shook my head slowly, thinking back on our lives on an island, so far away.

Alain let out a low whistle. "Well, I see you have taught her woodworking. She is doing well."

Anne arrived in the doorway. "Hey, Dad. What are you doing?" She looked around the shop at ancient tools furred with dust stuck to grease. She said to Alain, "What a mess. How come this boatyard is such a dump anyway?"

Alain blinked. He considered. "Ah, why. Why? Two things: one is the Paco Torres family and the other is Grandfather."

We waited.

He said, "The Torres family had worked for us for generations. Paco and my grandfather worked in the yard before the war. After the war, Paco had joined the communists. Grandfather worked for De Gaulle's French Resistance. They became enemies. Paco was exposed as a Nazi collaborator and went into hiding. His nephew, Jose Ignacio, took over as head of the yard crew of uncles, cousins, and later, sons. As a small boy, raised by Grandfather, I watched the Torres family steal from our yard. I did not realize it at the time—what it was they were doing. In my family one never questions adults.

"As was the custom in my family, I was sent away to school in England for many years. When I returned, I tried to modernize the business. I found there had been many losses. Fishing was disappearing in the Mediterranean. I tried to bring in classic yachts and pleasure cruisers. The Torres family refused change. I caught them stealing again, and this time, I reported to Grandfather. He was very angry with me! I took him to the warehouse where the crew kept all the stolen goods. Grandfather confronted Jose Ignacio; Jose became crazy-angry. He swore to destroy me, Grandfather, and the yard. Then, he and his family quit. To this day Grandfather is angry with me. He is angry with the Torres family, for he feels that Paco, his enemy, was behind all of this. And Jose Ignacio told Grandfather that they all believe he was the one who turned in Paco as a collaborator. Very bad. The Torres crew disappeared across the border to Catalonia.

And I got disinherited. After that, Grandfather would sit for days with *Marie Celine*, drink wine, smoke, listen to the transistor radio, tuned always to the *nostalgie* station, and read his old memoirs. Very sad." He looked down, pursing his lips.

Anne asked, "Is that the Paco dude who's responsible for Jeanine's mother's death? And Rod's arrest?"

"Yes, Anne, the same."

"He is a really scary person," Anne said. "He dare not cross our border."

"Your borders are all open now," I said. "Who would know if he came back?"

Alain looked mystified. "Even I would not know. I have never seen Paco Torres—except when he was young—in old photographs. No. Do not worry. Such an evil person. Such evil coming back to haunt us? No. All that is in the past."

Then he brightened. "It must be time to eat. I am very hungry."

We three went back into the boathouse. As I walked along, I thought about that Paco Torres. For a second, I felt the chill of a dark wind blow over me. I decided not to mention my thoughts to anyone. But I had a deep sense of uneasiness.

Louis had arrived with food. We moved over to the picnic area. Oh, lovely food. Alain sat by Pierre. Both of them were cautious, like two dogs scratching, sniffing, circling.

There was a terrible noise of beating metal and shouts coming from the gates. "What's that?" Pierre yelled to no one in particular.

Eric, just arrived, in starched white coveralls, sat at the end of the table with two of his young mechanics. "Protesters. Out at the main gate there are even more protesters." His look was worried. "They swarmed around our truck when we brought the new engine parts into the yard. Many of them are merely young ruffians."

"Bastards," Pierre cried. "Did they attempt to get inside the yard?"

"No way." Graydon's voice rang over the table. He trundled up to the luncheon area laden with cameras, sound equipment, and two long-haired, black-T-shirted cameramen. "We turned the cameras on them and they split."

Pierre said, "What do you mean, 'split'?" He motioned for Graydon and crew to sit and eat.

"They fled. *S'enfuir!*" Graydon said, unloading his packs and rubbing his hands gleefully over the display of Provençal cuisine before him. "I'm making my own documentary."

"Wonderful, Graydon," I said, thinking to myself, no one can attack us, or any such thing, without him filming it. Still, I could hear muffled shouts from the group outside the yard. We toned down to whispers. Pierre raised his voice, "Most assuredly, there can be no real problem." The conversation drifted into the progress on replacing the tools destroyed in the fire.

Pierre blustered up, "We will get all these tools again. I promise. Let us speak of pleasant things! The masts will be ready for the rigging and sails, but of course, this is so." He looked at Alain, hopefully.

Everybody waited while Alain sat looking at his grandfather, perplexed. "Sails." He said this as if he were disoriented. "Where are the sails, Grandfather?"

"Ah," Pierre said this to the table, "where they are supposed to be, with the rest of the gear for our Angel Ship. In the big shed, of course!"

Alain looked at his grandfather. "I did not see them in the big shed."

"We go!" Pierre ordered. Alain and Pierre left the table.

TWENTY-ONE

Back in Time

*U*NEASY, WE NIBBLED our food and waited. I had an idea forming while waiting. It had been very hard, with my new memories coming to me bit by bit, to actually force my mind to go back to one point in the past. It was a new feeling to be able to step back to the past at will. To have a past! I really had to recall clearly, back to places and people I had just recently rediscovered. I had to go to the beginning of *Marie Celine*.

Alain and Pierre returned dejected. "No sails," Pierre whispered hoarsely. "They may have been in the sail loft."

"Grandfather! Who would put them there? We have not had a sail-maker since I was a young boy!"

"Perhaps the old crew placed…" Pierre started.

"I cannot believe this! This is terrible! The sails for a schooner! Many sails! The money!" Alain was maddened with shame and frustration, embarrassed that this occurred before us. "How can this happen with such a glorious, magnificent ship?"

Before Pierre and his grandson could get into a row, I put in, "We will manage the money somehow. What we really need is a sail plan. Get new sails made up."

Graydon and I had discovered my old boatyard, Philip and Son, was now defunct and a new marina had been built in her place. I knew that most of the people in the nearby town of Dartmouth had been employed by the yard for generations. There had to be someone who remembered my father and the boat. Someone who would know where they used to have the sails made.

I continued, "Give me a little time. I think I can find a sail plan." I moved to the end of the table. "Graydon, can you come with me and bring your computer?"

In M. Riquet's office, Graydon and I found the phone numbers for the new marina. After a few blunders, I did connect with one of the marina owners who sounded rather harried and impatient. I told him we needed information about the old boatyard and I explained our mission. There was a long pause at the other end. At once, he became keen. "I say, I have been reading about your mission in the papers. A Little Ship is she? Built here."

"Yes. Yes, indeed."

"I believe I know a chap from your day. He, his father, and his brothers worked in the boatyard. They were the third generation from that Dartmouth family. He was the youngest of that clan to work there. I'll collect my partner, hold on a moment..." I heard him conversing with a couple of other men. He got back on the line. "We've looked him up, Mr. Neville. And good luck to you."

The manager gave me the name Jack Williams, and his number.

My hands were shaking as I dialled. The name, Jack Williams, sounded familiar. A deep whiskey voice answered. "Williams on this end."

I explained who I was and my mission. Again, there was a long silence; I thought the line had gone dead. "I say, is anyone there?"

A low chuckle came from the other end. "You're the nipper that hung about the yard! We all tended to you when your mum and dad worked on the boat."

I could hear his smile. "I believe so." It all came back. He used to pull me around the yard in the dock cart. He was older than I, but not by much. He tagged after his brothers as they worked. I tagged after him. "And you pestered Mum for the muffins she baked on the cook stove. I was afraid you would eat my share!"

We camped under the boat for months at a time. The cook stove eventually went in the boat. Wet and miserable in foul weather, I can't remember such fun. Such happiness. Mine again. As I listened to Jack go on, I heard myself laughing, tears running down my face. Graydon put his arm around me. Dear man.

"I lived for your mum's oatcakes. Made in the skillet? Your mum was some cook!"

"And Dad?"

"Oh lord, Dr. Neville was my hero. A hero of the boatyard, as well, you know. People came from all round England to get knowledge from him. He not only helped build the boats he designed, and worked as a doctor in town, he took the time to show me and my brothers tricks to boat building you'd never find in a book or school. Oh, a gentle, patient man he was, with us kids. A giant of a man to us. We used to envy you, Colley, camping out like cowboys and Indians. Colley, you remember the coach whipping on the tie rod? Up in the forepeak?"

I did. It was beautiful workmanship.

"Your dad taught me that rope work!"

"Jack, it's still there. Getting a new coat of white paint by my sister."

To be so close to Dad and Mum again was life-giving. I could smell the yard, the iron-working section, smoke of coal, smouldering metal, the wooden boat portion, wood smoke as the ribs and planks were steamed into shape, wood shavings, paint, saws buzzing. It was home. It was safe. It was mine again. And watching *Marie Celine* grow into a beautiful ship. Oh my, I do know heaven.

Jack told me about the bombing in 1942. How he lost twenty-two mates. How all the yacht records and buildings were gone.

"Jack, I wonder, can you remember where we got the sails made for the *Marie Celine*?"

"Your father had all his boats' sails made up north somewhere.

Would not consider any other sail loft. I can't recall the name…let me get the missus. She worked in the office." A few long moments and Jack came back. "G. Butler and Son. How in the hell did I forget that name? Think I was getting on in age, wouldn't you? They're up in Cowes, Isle of Wight. Good luck, Colley. Me and the missus will try to get to the Little Ships to cast you off."

I rung off, and Graydon and I found the numbers for G. Butler and Son. It was still in business. Again, my hands were shaky as I dialled. I mis-dialled. All those numbers, country codes and what. My palms were too wet. Graydon dialled for me. He connected and handed the phone to me. It was quite easy, at first. I got an office clerk who listened to my story and handed me over to a Mr. Butler. His fresh young voice told me that he would not relate to the story of my dad and *Marie Celine*. He listened and went quiet. Again I was left feeling as though I had been disengaged. He came back on. "Mr. Neville, I am sending you on to my grandfather, Mr. Butler. Please hold on a bit."

A slow-speaking, gentle voice came on the line. "Butler here. My grandson told me you have an interesting story."

Again, I told of my dad and the Little Ships. At the end I said, "Mr. Butler, do you still have a library of sail plans?"

"Yes." Then he said no more.

Then I said, "Mr. Butler, is there a chance you could still have the sail plan for *Marie Celine*?"

"Could be a chance. Could be." He said this with uncertainty.

"Mr. Butler, I wonder…could you help us find the sail plan?"

Mr. Butler sounded more lively and chuckled on the other end. " Well, young Neville, I don't do much these days but pet the cat and stoke the stove." He chuckled again.

I felt I was losing the last little thread I had to the sails. Mr. Butler sounded as though he did not have both oars in the water. To make a new plan would be expensive and take time. Too much time.

Then he woke up. "Mr. Neville, was your father the Dr. Richard Neville? Boat designer?"

I said yes. I was sure I had told him that. I heard him humming a tune and the shuffling of shoes on a wooden floor. He spoke up, "We have one of the biggest libraries of sail plans in the United Kingdom. Give us a bit of time, and I will get back with you. If I can't find the sail plan, then you will have to give me all the specs on your boat and we will make one up."

"We don't have much time, Mr. Butler."

We exchanged contact information. By this time, the whole crew had left the boatyard and crowded into M. Riquet's office. I needed Pierre and Alain most, for they were the last to sail her. To afford a whole suit of sails would have been prohibitive. Pierre, Alain, Eric, Mal, Rutherford and I gathered at a table in the dining room to decide which sails were absolutely essential for this trip. Later we could add the rest.

A staysail schooner with a simple Marconi rig, such as ours, has a mainsail, a main staysail, a jumbo before the foremast (the largest jib) then a jib, and a triangular topsail, called a fisherman's staysail, which can catch a lot of wind on light-air day. We decided to go with the bare minimum: a mainsail, main staysail and jumbo. No jib. No fisherman's.

At times, the discussion became a bit tense. Rutherford in his donnish manner proclaimed, "She won't be properly dressed out. That will never, never do."

Irritated, I asked, "How did you reach that conclusion, Rutherford?"

"Obviously, Neville, it's in all the books on classic yachts."

Mal chimed in, "As a navy man, I agree with Rutherford. We should be proper Bristol-bloody-fashion."

"She will be easier to manage without those extra sails," I offered.

"Poof!" Pierre's cheeks ballooned out with each indignant poof. "We must have all the sails flying. Look proud. Poof!"

"Grandfather, we have to take it slow. Those extra sails will make her hard to handle and too fast."

"Poof! I cannot believe my grandson will say such a thing. What if we have no wind? We need the fisherman's!"

"We must consider the cost, Pierre!" I urged.

Louis padded up and said in his soft voice, "We could motor only. No sails are needed with a motor." Everybody stared in amazement at Louis, as he slunk into the background.

The phone rang, jolting us. Mr. Riquet hurried in, fussing, "It is the sail people!" I looked over the crew. Pierre gave a slow grave nod. "We must reduce the sails." The rest agreed and ran to join me in the office. Mr. Butler senior was on the line.

"Young Neville, we have your sail plan. We can get these out in about a fortnight, maybe less, if we put the whole loft crew on it." He sounded surprisingly alert, even excited.

Embarrassed, I had to explain the sail reduction. "Yes, we really don't need those other sails for this trip." I said this with forced cheeriness.

"I can't imagine *Marie Celine* without all sails up, in fine form, crossing the Channel with the Little Ships."

I felt that he could hear me blush. I let out a long sigh. "Well...I am sure everything will be tickety-boo, even with the smaller suit of sails." I asked him the price and gave my crew a brave, reassuring smile, for the price was astronomical. I cleared my throat and asked him the amount for a deposit and said that we would wire it. To my astonishment he said, "No deposit from our old clients."

"Well, young Neville, I trust all will be well. I will contact you soon." He rang off.

All of us gathered, including Graydon, to hear the news. Already we had used most of our funds, and there were still many more expenses and the transport truck to be found. A glum group, we sat in momentary silence.

Graydon spoke up. "Listen guys, Louis is right. Why can't you motor across the Channel?"

"Graydon! That's unacceptable. The motor will be on, naturally. It was used the entire evacuation, but the sails were up as well! *Marie* must sail across the Channel! She's been reborn. She is a symbol of endurance and victory." I was shocked our Graydon would say such an insensitive thing. I said, "We can do this. We can sail her across the Channel. We will get those sails."

"We will, by God." Pierre slammed his hands on the table.

The others acquiesced, but there was a ripple of reservation in the background.

TWENTY-TWO

Will Not Be Defeated

*L*ATER THAT DAY, Pierre rushed into the boathouse and slammed the doors. He was splotched with rotten tomatoes. "Communists! Hooligans! Savages! Every day in this village they laugh. Laugh! They say we old ones will never get this boat finished. They say we will never take her to England." He stood before the boat, his face hardened into a long, deep frown of hurt, pain and anger; then he went along the boat running his hands down her sides, patting her gently. For an instant it seemed the life had run out of him and he was suddenly a very old man. Head bent, shoulders slumped, he swept his hands along her hull and stumped along her side like a blind man.

"Pierre! Captain Pierre Jeantot. Free French!" I yelled. "We will not be defeated!"

Abruptly, he stopped. His back straightened, stiffened as if he had been struck. He turned slowly and considered me. "No! No! No! We will not be defeated. *Marie* has come back to life. So have we. I will not fail her. I will not fail you, my friends." His face lifted and opened with new determination, energy. "Now, we go to work."

And work we did. Every morning, heads high, we marched past the milling protesters at the gates. We worked all day and into the night to ready *Marie* for her journey.

One morning, I arrived at the boathouse to find Graydon was happily filming our tasks for his documentary. Alain had worked through to morning after the oak stock arrived. We never saw him. He fashioned a perfect stem and installed it. No one would ever guess it had not been the original. Eric had the engine in prime condition, the fuel tank replaced, all new lines and filters, and finally a new paint job. One could eat meals off that engine.

The women finished the interior and it was smashing. The forest-green interior canvas with cream piping was installed throughout the cabins and saloon with pillows of complementary colours. New bunk mattresses were installed and covered with interior canvas. All brass and bronze had been polished, and the cabin sole sanded out and refinished with a rubbed varnish; bulkheads and raised panelling all got coats of new varnish. The boat once more smelled new and clean. She was an angel, my *Marie Celine*.

Marie's seams were caulked, filled and faired. We were painting the last coat of pearl-white finish on the hull. The decks were ready with coats of oil that brought out the butternut colour of the teak. We were working to our full capacity, yet we still had a lot to do before we could get her in the water. I feared we would still be in France when the Little Ships sailed.

Later in the fury of work, I took a break and carried two bottles of beer over to Alain's work area in the shed outside the boathouse. Anne was laying on the sixth coat of varnish on the masts. The varnish layers looked like golden syrup in the sunlight. "Look, Dad, I can see my image in this varnish! Wow! So bright."

"Perhaps that's why they call it 'bright work,'" I said, admiring her accomplishment, and asked about Alain.

"In the shed getting the hardware for the rigging," she said.

Inside, adjusting my eyes to the dim light, I spied Alain uncoiling rolls of wire rigging that was black with dirt. Boxes of bronze turnbuckles, tangs, toggles, blocks and cotter pins—green with age—were placed on the floor, next to bottles of vinegar used for cleaning. Alain did not notice me at first. "Well, chappy," I said lightly, "anything salvageable?" I handed him a bottle.

He took a long pull on his beer and gave me a brave smile that looked to me more like a grimace. "But yes, Mr. Neville, surely we can make this work. It will get us across the Channel. I will splice some new rope to the wire in places. She will be fine. The masts will be rigged in no time!" Again, I was to discover that Alain worked into the nights remaining.

TWENTY-THREE

Splash

*T*ODAY WE WERE to put *Marie* in the water. Early morning, all of us were downstairs, dressed and anxious. Graydon's camera darted about us like a mosquito. Jeanine and Rod were already taking coffee. Outside, the brilliance of the mica-white sunlight of Provence amplified the robin-egg sky and touched the leaves of the plane trees green-gold; it turned the dull, gravelled petanque courts across the street a vitreous tan.

Our energy buzzed around the breakfast table: excitement, anticipation, and quite a bit of fear. We all had the same realizations. What happened if the engine failed? What if *Marie* took a fall going off the ways? What if *Marie* broke a rib? What if *Marie's* planks took in water too fast for the pumps? *Marie* could sink. It had been too many years that she was left high and dry in this hot climate.

The rest of our crew was waiting at the boathouse in a disarray of cigarettes, coffees, *pichets*, tumblers of wine, and chunks of bread. They all had that wide-eyed startled look that I am sure mirrored my group. It was either a first date or a firing squad.

Pierre and I stepped up. We gave orders and got cracking. Last-minute checks of engine, sea cocks, bilge pumps, batteries, planks, seams, keel, and keel bolts.

We took our posts. After many practice sessions with Pierre and Alain, the women were readied out on the dock to catch lines as *Marie* entered the water. Rod and I, Rutherford and Mal were on the lines inside. Alain manned the power winch that held the cables to the cradle. Louis, Eric, and Pierre stood by. After nearly losing her before on this track, we all were extremely tense. This time it had to go right.

Clunk, clug, whine went the cable as its engine fired, smoking. Alain manned the brake and let *Marie* move inch by inch down the railway. She reached the water at the bottom of the ramp, still on a steep angle, her stern tipping sharply; she looked as if she wanted to knife too fast into the water, submerging that fine stern and possibly breaking it. Then she could thrust out like a javelin, landing randomly atop surrounding piers and boats.

We held a collective breath. No sound could be heard save the screech of the pulley. She strained on the ropes. At the last second her stern began to float and bobbed up. Alain shut down the cable and ran to board the boat. With a sigh, *Marie* slid graceful as a swan into the water, making a swell as she landed. Alain heaved lines to the women, who pulled her back and made her fast to the dock.

Eric jumped aboard and went below. We waited. The engine thunked. Once. Twice. Three times. We listened. We waited. We watched. On the fourth try, the engine turned over. Black smoke puffed out the exhaust. Then, the good sign: water pumped out the exhaust. A cheer rose up from the docks. The engine's steady chuntering was music to all of us.

We crowded the dock, hugging, cheering, kissing. Alain moved amidst the celebrating crew, wildly happy. He grabbed, hugged, and kissed his grandfather several times, to the extent that Pierre laughed surprised, truly amazed, water glassing his eyes. Pierre caught up with me, paused, then gave me a hug and a kiss on both cheeks. Alain moved through the group, hugging, kissing, and bumped into Anne. Without pausing, he bent down and folded her into an exuberant embrace, lifting her off the ground. I saw her startled face appear over his shoulder, her eyes wide with perplexity.

As expected, the bilge pumps turned on, plus two shore pumps. Monitoring the pumps, we, the crew of *Marie Celine*, spent the remainder of the day washing her down, polishing brass and bronze. She was stunning in the water, floating gently on her lines in the current.

Working down below, tears pricked and stung behind my eyes as I looked over my childhood home. In the main stateroom, where my parents had slept, the double bunk was elegantly done with flowered comforter and matching shams and curtains. The photos of our family were still screwed to the bulkhead, but the frames and glass were new. The restored interior was nearly identical to the old edition, except a bit more cozy. I knew Mum and Dad were watching. I knew Mum would like it. I could feel their presence. Yes…they assured me they liked it very much. I nodded, pleased with their attention on the subject, their approval.

"Oh, Colley, she looks ever-so lovely!"

I closed my eyes, "Mum?"

It was Lizbeth. I sucked in a deep breath. "Damn, Lizbeth! I feel quite the fool. You must think I'm bonkers. Dear Liz…it is simply years of conversing with ghosts, I suppose. It is somewhat…"

Lizbeth hooked her arm in mine and gave me a squeeze. "I know, Colley. Out in the Northern Territories, alone in the white, white world there, I had splendid conversations with my father, my mother and, of course, Gran. My ghosts, as you call them, were my constant companions, and I may say, far more companionable than my colleagues." She paused and listened, closing her eyes and raising her brows. "Your mum's here, Colley love. I feel her too." Lizbeth hooked her arm around my waist and pulled me into her stolid, ample warmth. We stood there, Liz and I, silenced by a current surging between us, like a restless spirit, moving from me to her and back again.

* * * *

Alain and I met at the boat at midnight, relieving Rod from pump watch. Water was still coming in, which was worrisome, but not unexpected. We went below into the lantern-lit, homey galley. Cheeses, breads, thermoses of tea, coffee, and a fortifying soup made from port wine and beef bouillon were set out on the drainboard. Bedding had been arranged for each watch; we made up our beds on the settees in the main saloon. With a cup of that wonderful soup, I settled in and looked around at the polished mahogany dining table, the Dutch-tiled fireplace, the blue and white tiles in the galley, and smelled wood and varnish, brass polish and tile polish. Even the hum of the bilge pumps splashing water overboard was comforting.

"Mr. Neville, this is a dream come true for me. Every day I imagined her finished and how she would look." Alain turned his lamp low and sat propped up on pillows with bit of brandy. "I never gave up. I knew someday she would be brought back to life. Only in my dreams, I alone saved *Marie*." I could see a wistful smile on his handsome face.

"I felt that way too, Alain. I imagined being her white knight and saving her from a horrible death. That dream kept me alive. Now I see she has that effect upon many people. She has touched the lives of us all. I think she brought us together in her spectral scheme of things."

Alain sighed, relaxed, lazy. "Yes. This I believe also. I did not capture her, she captured me...captured all of us."

"Alain, I hope you are not too awfully disappointed that we all turned up in your dream...Alain?"

His empty glass tipped against his chest, his eyes were closed, and the look on his face was serene. I rose, removed the glass and turned off his oil lamp. Letting myself down into my bunk, I opened my book and turned down my lamp. I was very safe, a child at home. Once in a great while, one really can go home again, in this the best possible world.

TWENTY-FOUR

Bundles from Heaven

*T*HE NEXT MORNING, I woke to noisy activity on the dock. Alain sat up in his bunk while I popped my head out the hatch. Alain's head came up next to mine. There, lined up on the dock alongside the boat were three men. One, quite old, with white hair and a red beard; the second, tall and sturdy, middle aged, his white hair streaked with red strands. The third man was young, about Alain's age, with a flaming red mop of hair and a smooth ruddy complexion.

"Ahoy there," the older man called. "Butler, Butler, and Butler, here! We've got your sails!"

Alain looked at them and then to me he whispered, "Do we have the money yet?"

"No," I said, "it's Sunday. The banks are closed. Hell." And to them I called, as I opened the hatch and climbed up the steps, "Please come aboard!"

And they did. We gave them a tour of the decks, below decks, and the masts. George Butler Senior and his son and grandson were greatly impressed. The elder more so.

"I remembered Dr. Neville's boats. My father was the one who fitted the sails for his boats, you see. And this one is the gem of them all. What an absolute beauty she is."

By this time, Pierre and the others were there with us. What a proud lot we were. Back at the boathouse, Louis laid out refreshments, and we opened the barn doors, while George Butler Senior backed their small van into the boathouse. Pierre and I helped unload the sail bags. Those bags may as well have been filled with pink diamonds for all the care and concern that went into moving them. Precious bundles sent from heaven. Pierre looked up at me, a cigarette dangling from his mouth and one eye closed from the smoke. "I count five. Five! Do you count five? Colley?"

I stood scratching my three-day's growth. "Indeed. I count five. Damn."

"Five it is," said George Butler Senior. "We couldn't let her go without her fisherman and jib." The other Butlers nodded, "Surely not, surely not."

Pierre's eyebrows lifted to me and his face stiffened into a sheepish grin. He whispered to me, covering it by a cough, "We don't have all the money yet."

I scratched my face again and addressed George Butler Senior. "We did not expect you chaps to finish so soon. To bring the sails here, such an honour and surprise. We thought we were meeting you in Dover to fit the sails."

"Meet in Dover, we will. And fit the sails, we will," replied George Butler Senior, "but we couldn't wait another moment to give you these sails and see the *Marie*. It has been a pleasure. Besides, we didn't want to take a chance on anything going wrong, you know. You have the sails, safe and sound with the boat."

I cleared my throat and looked to Pierre; his face was frozen in that smile. So, I said to the Butlers, "You must stay and be our guests." My mind was racing: *What the hell are we going to do? And the extra cost of two more sails!*

George Butler Senior laughed, "With pleasure. But we must leave very early in the morning. Work is backing up, you know."

It was a most enjoyable evening. And in the morning the Butlers were preparing to leave when Pierre said, "We must wait for the banks to open, Mr. Butler." Pierre's voice was tight, striving to sound light, casual.

Butler Senior laughed. "We don't need the bank to open. We're do-nating these sails to *Marie Celine*, the Little Ship of Dunkirk. We had to do our bit, you know. She helped us win the war." And Butler, But-ler, and Butler headed out the door. George Butler Senior called back, "See you in Dover. Fair winds and God bless."

* * * *

Everything was ready, except two most important things. One, we had to wait until *Marie's* planks swelled; so far the pumps were still going and time was running out. And two, we had no boat transport!

With this we had some trouble. When Pierre was attempting to ab-scond with the boat, Eric had borrowed a flatbed, but it was not prop-erly rigged to carry a wooden boat any distance. He had nothing modern and low to the ground, with the special springs that are needed to cushion the ride of a wooden boat. He had been searching, ready to beg, borrow, or steal a newly equipped boat transport. We had to get this old boat down the French highways, through the tunnel to the English traffic, which I heard was terrifying, and on to Dover. We were all becoming despondent as the days ticked by. The deadline was near-ing, with no lorry and the pumps still going.

Just days before we had to depart for England, we got a call from Eric. He was in Paris. There might be the rig we needed, just outside of the city. He had to make a few arrangements, but he felt hopeful. We waited. Early morning two days later, the front gates opened and Eric's transport rolled into the yard. The Mercedes diesel whistled and roared like a jet engine. The cab was painted metallic in the French tri-colours of blue, white and red. Our crew gathered around to admire the long, low flatbed, inches from the ground. It looked like a lean bat-tle ship. Eric jumped down from the cab, boasting, "This baby, she can take on anything. Yes, even English drivers!"

Pierre hurried up next to Eric, fretting, "Eric! How can you afford this, my friend?"

Eric's tiger-eyes flashed. "This is a birthday present for the gallant

Marie. She saved us once, you know. She deserves the best! Besides, my captain, this is not a new machine. But she is in good shape, and she will add to the business." Pierre hugged Eric and kissed him on both cheeks and hugged and kissed him again. Eric turned away, brushing off the attention.

The skies were pewter and clotted with rain clouds; some sprinkles had already begun. We went down below. Mal, Rutherford, Pierre, Eric, Louis and I all slid comfortably around the big dining table. Lizbeth, Jeanine, Anne and Cici were busy in the galley stowing Mum's cooking utensils found in the storage shed.

Lizbeth slid on the settee next to me. "Love, we're ready on our end."

Jeanine interrupted, "Except this one pot. This pot is not fitting anywhere! It covers three burners on the stove. Too big. Perhaps it was not supposed to be with the boat inventory." She held it up. "Should we chuck it?" There was a loud "Noooo!" from all of us who knew that large pot.

Jeanine, perplexed and a bit annoyed, set it down on the counter. Cici and Lizbeth stared at us peevishly.

We all spoke at once. Mal blasted out, "That's the pot that fed hundreds of the BEF off the beaches. Nearly dead they were, and that pot made a stew that brought them back to life."

Rutherford: "Right-oh, I'll never forget that smell of mutton. And Dr. Neville ladling the stuff out to the soldiers; some took it in their helmets and…" Then quickly, he said, "Sorry, didn't mean mutton was lowly, chappies. It's just, you see, it was all so awfully incongruous… the blood and mutton on the decks, the dying men and the food of their farms, and villages, and mums' kitchens coming to them in such a hellish place. To save them…you see."

I nodded. Around the table, we, the survivors, were lost in a collective memory. Mutton, blood, and Dunkirk sand on the decks. Over 300,000 British Expeditionary soldiers, saved from the beaches of Dunkirk by Little Ships, and we all felt saved by a bit of Mum's mutton stew, as well.

Louis said, "That's the pot that saved us from starvation when we boarded *Marie* from our march to the beaches. We had had no food. Brandy and cigarettes had been our food for weeks. We thought we were dying. That pot of English stew saved us!"

Rod broke in, "Blimey, it was the best mutton I ever had in me life!"

The women took another look at the large stockpot. I explained, "It was not part of our stores on the boat. Mum borrowed it from the village pub before we departed for Dunkirk." I added, "It must stay on the boat somewhere, even in the chain locker. For good luck. That cooking pot is a symbol of survival. For all times." The others agreed.

We passed Louis's pizzas around the table. And filled our glasses. Cici said in a high hushed voice, "Listen!" her eyes wide. We listened. At once, we cheered. The bilge pumps had stopped. We opened the cabin sole and checked the bilge. Dry! Yes!

"We go!" Pierre yelled.

TWENTY-FIVE

The Road to Dover

*A*T DAWN, WE packed the new sails and tools into the saloon for the trip. By sunrise, we had moved *Marie* up the channel and into one of the slipways, lifted her out of the water with the travel lift and set her gently on the flatbed cradles. Her masts were tied alongside. She was a majestic sight, varnish glistening in the rising sun, her classic pearl-white hull reflecting pink clouds. Eric walked the perimeter of the flatbed, testing lashings.

Jeanine glided by wearing baggy black trousers with suspenders, a white peasant blouse and a black beret. She gave a little smile, "It still fits—my uniform in the Resistance—Colley. Imagine!" Rod appeared at her side; he had squeezed into his recently altered British army uniform. We had drawn straws on who was going to ride in the cab with Eric; the Slaters won. Eric fired up the engine. We cheered. Gathering our bags, we clamoured into waiting Eurovans, one owned and driven by M. Riquet, the other rented and driven by Graydon. Both were equipped with legal running lights and signs for escorting an oversized load down the highways of France and England. Taking up the rear, Anne, Alain, Lizbeth, Pierre and I rode with Graydon. Heading the caravan, Cici, Rutherford, Mal and Louis rode with Riquet. There was a third van with Graydon's technicians and camera equipment.

Our caravan was ready. Front gates were opened and the lorry inched forward, careful not to jolt *Marie*. We followed. As soon as the lorry was outside the gates, the brake lights went on.

We couldn't see around the boat. Pierre and I debarked and were joined by Mal and Rutherford. We went up to the side of the cab where Eric and Rod waited. Pierre, Rod, and Eric fell into hot conference. Alain came to my side, along with Anne, Jeanine, and Lizbeth.

We faced a mob of elderly vets and local people, augmented by young bodgies from surrounding villages. They carried banners and signs painted with epithets: capitalist dogs, Gaullists, royalists, traitors. The pack inched forward. Alain pointed out the Torres family in front, shaking fists and inciting the others. In front of them was a short, thickset old man in a black, hooded sweatshirt under a worn leather jacket. He had a patchy, iron-grey beard, and dark grey hair fringed the hood. What I could see of his face was parched olive skin, almost the colour of the mottled jacket he wore. What caught me were his eyes. Against the hood and complexion, his eyes were hazel and they shone with a feverish brightness. He was oddly still amidst this animated mob. A warning bell rang in my body.

I was acutely aware of the situation. Standing off in the background were policemen at attention and alert. The press was on location; lines of satellite vans were parked along the lanes. Graydon and his crew began counter-filming. Pierre, Rod and Eric, were still in conference.

Alain was close to me. I whispered, "Do you know who that is?" I slid my eyes toward the hooded man.

Alain stole a glance. "There is something familiar about him…"

Jeanine grabbed my arm and whispered, panic shrilling her voice, "That is Paco Torres! There is going to be a fight. A bloody fight! What can we do?" Cici and Elizabeth put their arms around Jeanine protectively.

"Nothing, yet. Wait," I said. "Whatever we do, we must not let them win." I knew it would be only seconds before Pierre and Rod spied Paco.

I called Anne over. "I heard Jeanine, Dad. That monster…"

As calmly as possible, I said, "Annie, be as casual as you can. Fetch Graydon. Don't look at that Paco or anybody. Get Graydon."

When Graydon arrived, I gave him my instructions and he moved away from the scene.

My group joined Pierre, Rod, and Eric. The pack moved closer to us.

"Jesus," snarled Mal, "this has gone a bit far! I'm losing my patience with this rabble." He stepped up to the front and squared off, his bum leg a bit akimbo.

Pierre gasped. "This," he pressed hands on each side of his head, "this I do not understand!"

"What do we do?" cried Cici.

"Chaps, we start up our engines and run them through!" Rutherford, in his tweeds and Oxford tie, was ready for action.

"Right-oh," blared Mal. "Run them through! Bastards!"

"But, lads, some of them are such old sods," said Lizbeth, alarmed. "You might just do that …run them through!"

I stepped in. "We must be calm and get the hell out of here."

M. Riquet entered the huddle with an arm full of tabloids. He opened them and read to us in English. "Here, this one is out of Paris. It says, 'Famous communist Resistance heroes attempt to stop exploitation and annexation of French heritage ship by the English…'

"And here, an English tabloid! Oh God. It says, 'French Communists want to scuttle English war relic!'

"Another English tabloid, I read to you. There, it says, this bit here is a quote from an old English folk song: 'She'll never-never-sail, never-never sail, earl-ee in the morning…' Then it goes on to say, 'The recently discovered Unfound Ship, *Marie Celine*, is doomed to be held hostage and rot in a small French village…'"

"Holy shit!" Rod read over M. Riquet's shoulder. "Where in the hell did they get this crap? The whole damn country's going to be up in arms! We'll be the laughing stock of the world!"

"Liars!" Anne blurted as she squeezed in the circle hearing the news. She looked over the mob. "Losers!"

Most of the village was on the scene by now. Rainy mist thickened and drifted around us.

It was then that I saw Paco lower the hood, revealing his full, broad face, twisted into a mean smile. Rod and Pierre roared, "Paco!" and started for him.

The crowd stood very still. I grabbed Rod and Pierre and pulled them back, close to me. "That's what he wants! We'll lose everything if you attack him in front of all these people!" They tried to pull away. "Listen," I commanded, "he's baiting you. He wants a fight. We'll all end up in jail. We'll lose *Marie*."

Rod and Pierre trained their sights on Paco. I said, "Stop. Listen. I've got a plan. Trust me." They hesitated. At that instant the mob started to rumble and yell. I took Pierre's arm. "We've got to stop this." Distressed, I scanned the area for Graydon. Then I took Pierre by the arm, "Pierre, follow me."

Pierre and I climbed up on the side of the lorry. Eric followed. Louis, hesitant and shy, and never athletic, climbed up with the help of Eric. Rod monkey-climbed with his one good hand, his jigsaw face intimidating. I helped Mal. Quite agile, Rutherford made it up without trouble. We lined up. I was at one end, Pierre at the other. All of us at attention, with obvious war injuries, were puffed with pride and determination.

Jeanine handed up French and English flags we had bought to fly on our *Marie's* voyage with the Little Ships. We unfurled the flags. I held the English Union Jack, Pierre, the French Tricolour.

Rod translated for me as Pierre's voice rang out over the crowd. "We fought in the war to end war. Did we not?"

The mob murmured reluctant affirmations.

"We went to war to free our country and live free of oppression. Repression. To keep our way of life, our languages, our cultures. Is this not so?"

A shuffling and stronger assent.

I said through Rod, "This Angel Ship, *Marie*, and the other Little Ships, carried French soldiers, 95,000 French, and 240,000 English soldiers away from death. *Marie* made it possible for them to fight again. This little ship took you, the French, off the beaches of Dunkirk.

Then she saved our resistance fighters. All manner of fighters: Royalist, Communist, Spanish, Jewish, American, the Polish fighters. Many, many were saved by this gallant little angel! *Marie* did not ask, 'What party are you? What race? Religion? What country? What family? Do you have money?' No! She carried us all to safety. Helped us win the war."

Pierre continued, staring down Paco Torres, "We protest if we please. We worship as we please, or not. We speak our own language. We have kept our own cultures." He pointed at Paco, "And you, Paco Torres, Nazi collabourator, you informed on Jeanine Slater's mother, the famous Resistance agent, Madame Cormeau, who was arrested and shot. You informed on our brave English Resistance fighter, Rod Slater; the Nazis crippled Rod for life." To the crowd he said, "This man, Paco Torres, will do anything to destroy our freedom. He is here again to destroy our Angel Ship's mission, the courage, ethics and the nobility of mankind that she represents…"

Words burst from me, "Do you want to go with this devil, Paco Torres? Or do you want to keep faith in the Angel Ship. Keep hope that basic goodness prevails in man, after all."

We said at once, "Let our Angel Ship go!"

The crowd backed away from Paco. Paco stood alone. Defiant. A blue car pulled up and two plain-clothes men emerged with drawn guns. More police cars arrived, and the present police closed in on Paco. The Torres boys turned and ran. The men in plain clothes handcuffed Paco Torres and dragged him away. Graydon shot past the crowd and jumped up beside me. "It took a few phone calls, but we got him! That guy's toast!"

The crowd's feet crunched and scraped on the pea gravel as they formed whispering little groups.

The sun was obscured by clots of clouds. We veterans stood on the rail of the lorry. A few villagers fell away. Some of the crippled ones, aided by comrades, moved back. Some pushed off in wheelchairs. Even the young hooligans backed off. The crowd parted, lining each side of the road. "*Vive La France!*" a few called out uncertainly.

We made haste in our own erratic gaits for our vehicles, in pursuit of *Marie*. Her lorry eased into the first low gears and her pearly hull floated amid a sea of watchful but respectful villagers. *Marie* was on her way to England. In the front seat Pierre shook his head slowly and made a sign of the cross. "Now, we go."

"By God," I shouted, "we are going to England!"

TWENTY-SIX

On the Road to Dover, Again

OR THE TRIP, each vehicle was equipped with a walkie-talkie. A crackle, then a voice came on. "I wonder, chaps… Rutherford here, on this end…how do you think *Marie* feels about all of this? Over."

"Jolly good," Rod said. Jeanine was making agreeable mutterings in the background. "Over."

"She's thinking: *About bloody time!* Over." That was Mal. Cici shouted something rah-rah in the background.

Pierre replied, "You must ask our angel and listen! She will tell you. Over." There was a conspiratorial chuckle among us in the back of Graydon's van. Graydon gave a dubious smile in the rearview mirror. My wise Lizbeth hummed thoughtfully. Anne and Alain let down their defensive walls and grinned, each seemingly weighing individual secrets. I knew some of us had listened and heard *Marie Celine*, even my Anne. Dear Anne, who sat arms crossed, her shoulder pressed up against the window, trying not to touch Alain, who was smashed up right beside her on the small bench seat.

A soft rain slicked the roads. We watched it streaming off *Marie's* decks. On highway A7 heading toward Lyon, we joggled along behind the lorry. We meandered through the rocky Rhone Valley. Our caravan picked up speed after passing the rugged canyons and mountains lining the Rhone. From the front, Pierre set up notes and plans on the seat top. He and I busily drew out the procedures for putting the boat in the water on the other side of the Channel.

Lizbeth nodded off to sleep against me. Her cushy body felt curiously comforting, a familiar sense from the past, one of those senses of pleasure, the doctors had once told me, that do not leave the brain during years of amnesia.

Snippets of conversation from Anne and Alain pulled at my attention. I watched the two of them from the corner of my eye.

"That farm we just passed. It is famous for sweet butter, here in this region." Alain pointed out the window. "It is the food the cows eat, it is said, that makes the butter so sweet."

Anne glanced out the window and said, with the flippant air of an expert linguist, "Ah, *le beurre.*"

Alain's dimples deepened as he pursed his lips together, repressing a grin. He raised his brows to the heaven beyond the roof liner. "Anne. Please. Do not speak French. It is terrible. I am sorry. But it is most terrible. You need to listen to the music of the language."

By this time Pierre and I were idly eavesdropping. Pierre occasionally rolled his eyes to me in his peculiar, dramatic manner.

Anne jutted out her chin. "It's Parisian French. In Paris they would, like, hate your southern accent."

Alain smiled wryly. "Oh, would they?" Then, on a second thought, he asked, "Have you been to Paris?"

Frustrated and indignant: "No, stupid. You know that!"

Alain prompted, "Ah, yes! It had escaped me. Very well. Now, Anne? Say: *beurre* for me again."

Anne glowered at him and pronounced the word through tight lips. It sounded like burr.

Alain looked away; then he put his face very close to hers. "Anne, watch my mouth, use your mouth. The English, the Canadians, they talk through tight lips. The jaw does not move!

"The nose, the throat, the tongue, they do not move. Horrible! Watch me: *le beurre*..." Alain's resonant southern voice radiated throughout the van. His jaw pushed a bit forward, his lower lip pouted out, "*le beurre*...say it."

Forgetting herself, Anne watched Alain's mouth and pushed out her jaw, pushed out her lips, pouted out her bottom lip. Alain, with difficulty, held his pose. She came very close to his face and pronounced, "*Le beurre*..." But her lips curled up into a smile and she started giggling. Alain, his eyes emptied of all seriousness, blinked with gaiety.

At that second, an exclamation from Pierre and a disgusted "Oh shit!" from Graydon broke into the peace.

"Look! What is that before us? Accident? What?" Pierre was up against the dash, leaning his forehead on the front window. "I do not understand this!"

"Jesus." Graydon applied the brakes, coming right up on the rear bumper of the stopped lorry. He drew his mobile from his pocket, "Cameras. Roll your cameras. This could be the story telling how we missed the big event in England. How Colin Neville and *Marie Celine* waited sixty years for this moment, only to be fucked-over by a bunch of narrow-minded French guys."

I saw Eric's cab door fly open. Then I saw a ruffled policeman shaking his head and finger angrily, motioning for Eric to stay put. The door closed. We rolled down windows and leaned out in the drizzle as far as we could, trying to see the trouble. Ahead was one of those rest stops that bridge the highway. Police cars were everywhere with flashing lights, their colours surrealistically brilliant against the pewter sky. Traffic blocked both sides of the highway, sprouting limbs of waving arms with clenched fists. Crowds lined the walkway over the highway. Crowds lined each side of the road. Crowds clumped under the protection of the roadside buildings. What an uproar. Horns honking.

People shouting. Police had formed a line to keep the demonstrators off the roads. Other officers directed traffic. I caught a glimpse of news cameras, but could not discern whose.

"This is not an auto accident. This is a demonstration." Pierre leaned out further. "*Merde!* This is a riot!"

"Wow! A revolution! Are they going to throw cobblestones at us?" Anne said.

"Anne Neville! This is no time for jest!" I snapped at her with atypical impatience. I got on the walkie-talkie. It was all too much. I knew this was the end. What was it all for? Everyone was trying to babble into the mouthpieces at the same time. Eric had a good view from the cab, and he said the crowds were waving their arms wildly. And up in the lead car, M. Riquet broke in, describing what sounded like a riot.

"What are we going to do?" Lizbeth's frame filled the opposite window. "They'll turn us back. They will."

The kids and I had the same thought. Alain and Anne burst out, "They're going to hurt *Marie Celine*!" They clambered toward the door and hovered at my back. I straightened up, barring them. A policeman came up to Graydon's window. We hurled a barrage of questions at him in French and English. Holding up his hands, halting the fury of words, he spoke in a harried, but officious manner.

"What did he say?" Anne kept asking.

"To turn off the electronics. They're going to escort us through this mess. We're to have a police escort," Graydon announced, with studied forbearance, as he started up the van. "Great." He looked grim, as if he were driving into a firing squad. The walkie-talkies had gone quiet.

Graydon's mobile phone rang; he turned it off and snapped it closed.

The lorry's brake lights flickered on, then off, and the rig crept forward, carefully, so as not to upset our *Marie*. We rolled up windows and locked the doors. We listened to muffled shouts from the crowd and raindrops on the van roof. As we arrived at the edge of the lines of people, objects hurled through the air toward the boat. We all let out cries of alarm. Anne let out a painful shriek. Graydon stopped the van.

We were going to take the law into our own hands! "Hold on, I say, hold on…" Lizbeth ordered, as she peered over the seat between Pierre and Graydon. "They're throwing something…I can't quite see…"

Anne cried out, "Oh my God. It's flowers! They're throwing flowers!"

Bouquets of wildflowers, long-stemmed red, silver, white, and yellow roses, bouquets and wreaths of lavender and herbs, flew from the lines of people, and landed on *Marie*, and on our van. The crowd pressed into us as we crept by. We rolled down the windows and accepted flowers passed to us from women, men, children, all ages, producing a spectrum of bright colours, in slick rain coats, foul weather gear, umbrellas. They sang out, "*Vive la France*" and, "*Allez France*." "God save the Queen!" rang out as well. Many waved small French and British flags. A choir in the crowd sang *The Marseilles*; another sang out *God Save the Queen*.

Pierre made the sign of the cross and turned to us with his Gallic shrug, "It is the spirit of *Marie Celine*!"

Draped in wreaths and flowers, our caravan became a beautiful parade as we made our way toward Calais and the Channel Tunnel. Horns honked, people waved as we passed.

Alongside the highway, crowds came to cheer us on.

Acknowledgments

I AM EVER SO grateful to Captain Mark and Clare Williams in Sussex, UK, who launched me on this voyage, and who spent their precious time between work and kids to send curated material to my mailbox. An eternal thanks to Trina and Doug Baker, Riverside California, my anchors in life and art. Thanks to Michael Hunt, and the East Kent Maritime Museum, and The Association of of Dunkirk Little Ships for all the transcripts and historical records.

Additional gratitude goes to Editor Jean Jenkins, San Diego California, for her kind forbearance working with this neophyte, and to lovely Editor Elizabeth Pomada, San Francisco, California, for her gentle encouragement, and to you, Editor Sue Kashanski, Nova Scotia, for your crackling energy and belief in the story.

And to Captain Peter Davidson, my navigational star, my Polaris, without whom this could never have happened.

The Angel Ship
Historical References

The Association of Dunkirk Little Ships, http://www.adls.org.uk/t1/

The S O E in France, M.R.D. Foot, Her Majesty's Stationery Office, London, England

Transcripts from the Imperial War Museum, London, England

East Kent Maritime Museum transcripts and historical studies, Ramsgate, Kent, England

The Miracle of Dunkirk, Walter Lord

Ships That Saved an Army, Russell Plummer

The Sands of Dunkirk, Richard Collier

Retreat from Dunkirk, Douglas Williams

British Admiralty pilot and navigation charts for the Dover Strait and English Channel, 1940

British Admiralty sailing directions for the Dover Strait and English Channel, 1940

Charts of Approaches to Dunkerque (1932-1940), French Institut Géographique National, Saint-Mandé, France

About the Author

K J KENNELLY has worked both at sea and in wine country ashore, using her knowledge and experience to follow her dual passions of sailing and the production of fine wine. Both pursuits can be indulged in her home port of Nova Scotia.

www.hellgatepress.com